After Ilium

A Modern Tale

Stephen Swartz

ISBN-13: 978-1-939296-21-4
ISBN-10: 1-939296-21-8

Myrddin Publishing Group

www.myrddinpublishing.com

Cover Design by Ceri Clark

After Ilium

A Modern Tale

Stephen Swartz

After Ilium

CHAPTER 1

"Rage, O Goddess, sing the rage of Achilles, murderous, doomed, that cost the Achaeans so many losses, who sent down to the House of Death so many sturdy souls, the souls of great warriors, made their bodies carrion, food for dogs and birds, while the will of Zeus pushes ever to its end...."

The meaning of rage was becoming clear to him. His lips were dry and cracked as he mumbled, his mouth tasting of dust. And yet he was more concerned with his own fate than with those of ancient heroes, or remembering the opening words of Homer's epic poem.

Was he meant to be carrion, food for dogs and birds? Under the hot sun he soon could be. He just wanted to go home, see his mother and father again, one last time before he died. He did not want it all to end on a deserted coastal road in northwest Turkey. He did not want his broken body buried a few steps from where he would let go his final breath, only a short drive from the ruins of Ilium.

With eyes closed tightly against the gritty dirt, he saw mostly darkness. At the edges, bronze light tried to sneak inside. A cloud of dust hovered around him, collected by the tepid air and assigned guard duty. He felt his body pressed against the tire tracks in the dirt. The surface beneath him was warm, wet with his perspiration. And his blood, he suspected.

At that moment, a vibration rose under him, the ground shaking, growing stronger. He suddenly realized what was happening. He broke through his stupor and, at the last moment, summoned what energy remained in him and thrust his weakened body over onto his side.

His eyes popped open, immediately fell shut against the bright sunshine. The sun was hot on his face as the vibration continued. A rough noise grew in his ears. He knew he must go further. *One more time*, he urged himself, and rolled over again. Then again—and found himself dropping into a shallow ditch filled with the same beige dust that covered everything in this dry Mediterranean landscape.

A vehicle rumbled past him, seemed to halt. Its loud, banging engine gave him hope. It must be a bus—one of the regular routes that wound along the coastline. The bus waited a short distance away, its engine sputtering then settling into a harmonious rumble. He heard the door creak open and some people bound out, chattering. They ran to him, kicking up dust but blocking the sun with their bodies.

The men's voices were gruff, thickly accented, their breaths heavy as they pulled his body out of its spontaneous grave. They were careful as they laid him on the dirt road. He could no longer open his eyes because of the blinding sun overhead. He felt someone searching his pockets. Another person dripped water on his face and wiped it away with a gnarled hand. A thick finger with rough skin and a wart forced his mouth open and water followed—a warm, awful liquid he could not swallow.

Then he was floating, as though angels had gathered him in their arms to take him home. He kept his eyes shut, feeling the sun burning his face. Several hands lifted him into the air. He levitated over the dirt road—up the slope he had been about to mount before he collapsed—and into the welcome shadow of the bus. Voices, curious cackles, shot at him from the bus windows, words he could not recognize. He was taken aboard after some anxious discussion in the strange language, and the bus lurched into gear, backfiring as it pulled away.

Perhaps, with some good fortune, he might return home, even if it took years. If the gods would allow it. Just knowing he was on his way made his heart warm with hope. As his body fell limp against the floor of the bus, his lips, cracked and bleeding, twisted uncontrollably into a soft, thankful grin, a silly mask he could not control.

ᘓ

"Your name?" spoke a male voice outside the bandages.

He wasn't asleep, but he didn't know exactly where he was either. He felt bandages over his face, blocking his view of the world he awoke to. Feeling a bed beneath him and sniffing the medicinal scents around him, he guessed he was in a hospital or clinic. He took a deep breath, pulling himself into alertness, and tried to clear his head. Things did not feel right.

His first act was to see if his jaw would move. It wouldn't.

"It is wired," said the same voice. "You can speak, yes?"

He tried again. He could move his jaw a little, he discovered, but the bolt of pain he felt warned him not to do it again. Concerned, he raised his head off the pillow and felt all of the blood rush out of his brain, and fell back.

"It's on this side, under your ear," the man explained, and a fingertip tapped lightly on his jaw. "It will heal."

He wanted to say something, something profound, like "Thanks," but he feared the pain of opening his mouth.

"What's your name?" the man repeated.

"A—lex," he managed after some time testing how much pain he could endure. The name sounded familiar.

A chuckle followed. "*Aleksa*? Like El-Xandar, the Macedon, yes?"

He didn't know what the man was talking about at first. Gradually he understood that the man recognized he shared his name with Alexander the Great, who in 334 B.C. had conquered this region of the world, leading an army of 10,000 at the age of twenty. He wondered for a moment how he knew those facts. It had been part of his Senior Seminar, only a few weeks past, his third course on ancient Greek history. With all his reading, all his studies, he was becoming an expert on the subject. So he should have known better, he decided. He should have been out conquering something, instead of only writing about it in well-researched papers for college courses. He was out in the real world now, a world that did not care about him. He was lost in Turkey, he recalled as if waking from a dream, and instead of standing tall among heroes and gods, the land seemed to have conquered him.

"Where...?"

"This...aaa, place, here...Edremit Hospital," said the man. "You...American?"

Alex could not answer, being too afraid and in too much pain. He did not know of any town named Edremit. He waited for another punch to his gut, a slap to his face, or a knife cutting his belly. That's all he remembered.

"You a lucky boy." The man almost seemed to snicker.

Alex sure didn't feel so lucky. Why was this man asking him such stupid questions? He started to go off on the litany of his lucky breaks: the cool summer jobs at CyberAmerica, being high school salutatorian, getting into a good college, the Webber scholarship, vice-president of his fraternity, getting a first date with Suzie Meyer, their sexual episodes—well, that one time he got to third base, anyway. None of them was due to luck, he argued, hearing the echo of his proud parents' voices. It was his hard work, his dedication that—

"You alive, yes?" asked the man.

Alex wasn't sure about that but he would take the stranger's word for it. He felt too much pain to think for himself. He could not even see whom he was addressing, but he assured himself the man must be the doctor who bandaged his wounds. He tried to smile, not with his mouth and sore jaw, his cracked lips and straight teeth, but with his mind and spirit, hidden beneath the bandage that covered his eyes. From inside his gauzy fortress he could regroup and prepare to continue the campaign.

He listened to the man exit, detecting amusement in his voice.

Campaign? Alex wondered why the man had mentioned Alexander the Great. His head felt heavy, as though one of the Macedon's huge siege elephants was standing on him. But he was not on any campaign. He had already finished college. He was free. No more homework, no more tests. His head was about to explode. *Stop all this history stuff. School is finished.* It was one thing to be interested enough in something to study it and achieve a degree in the subject, called an expert, but it was very different to infuse one's daily life with everything one learned in four years of college. Now, with graduation almost two months behind him, what was he supposed to do with his life? No one who might hear him would understand anyway.

He suddenly felt a vague memory forming around the edges of his mind. He had been touring the site of ancient Troy, what historians call Ilium, when he lost his way. Yes, that seemed right. He was at Ilium. Now where was he? He felt as though he was in a dream: he had entered a classroom prepared to take the final exam and suddenly realized he had read the wrong books and did not get enough sleep the previous night. Moreover, the test was written in Turkish.

A degree in ancient history? What good is that?

Alex tried to sit up, wanting to get some assurance from the medical staff that he was not dreaming. A sharp stab of pain shot through his cheeks. Yet pain could be felt in a dream. The dull ache behind his eyes exploded into a sharp retort that rattled down his neck to the small of his back. He froze. Then screamed—using a mouth which could only mutter a moment before. He was not dreaming.

The doctor rushed in, touching his arm. He had a nurse give Alex an injection which left his head swimming and his body numb.

"You a bad boy, yes?" the doctor grilled him, almost with a chuckle.

Alex wondered what he meant.

"You have bad fall?" the doctor asked him and burst into laughter, which made Alex feel very uneasy, even as he slipped into a relaxed stupor.

If the doctor meant physically fall, like down a well, then no. He was not that clumsy. But a fall from grace, perhaps? That was not out of the question. If only he could *speak* to the doctor—to anybody.

Alex was still conscious enough to fear his present circumstances. He wanted to speak whole paragraphs to them, not just one or two grunted responses. There was a lot more he needed to tell them, even if they did not understand English very well. If he could just make them understand what had happened to him, maybe someone could do something. He did not belong here. It was all a mistake. What seemed like the next great thing in his life was a very bad mistake. He knew that now. In his pain, fear, and confusion, he simply wanted to go home.

He was not some clumsy oaf. He had not fallen down a well, as the doctor had surmised. He had not tripped over a small stone and land face-first into a ditch. He was certainly smart enough not to walk in front of a bus. Filled with anger, Alex could not relax, and that made his pain continue. The drug was weak, he decided. He still felt pain, lots of pain. Even as he tested the threshold, he understood that much of the pain he felt was not from his body, not from his head or his jaw, but from the wounds to his spirit.

Immobilized in the sweat-soaked hospital bed in a stale room without air conditioning, Alex suddenly believed he was not going to survive. He had a feeling in his gut that if he closed his eyes to sleep again that he might not awaken. His ears sharpened, listening to the noises around him, and outside the room—out the windows, people were plotting against him on the streets. Someone was after him, someone who wished to harm him. He could not even see anyone who might come up to attack him. He would have to listen carefully for footsteps, for breathing, and notice that person's scent.

The near-sickening perfume of the medicines and ointments merged with the spicy, greasy Turkish food being delivered to each patient, made him conjure an eerie world where gods and heroes continued playing their mythic games without any concern for the world. The ho-hum attitude of the staff, and the unnerving chuckles of his doctor, whom he was forced to rely on for any treatment and communication, made him think he was soon to be on his way down to Hades to mingle with its zombie hordes. The doctors and nurses who came and went seemed like denizens of the Underworld to him, faceless voices, touching him at random. In his mind, they condensed from opaque gray curtains, as though stepping on stage, and after making their case for his injuries, arguing that he deserved everything he got, they just as fluidly coalesced into the background.

His mind was spinning out of control, the drugs taking effect. When they wore off, they were injected again. How many days had it been since he had set out to visit Ilium, the site of the ten-year siege of Troy? It was three thousand years earlier, yet this dusty, dried-out, strangely fragrant land with its exotic charms and hidden dangers was the same—strangely the same.

What alarmed him most about his situation was his realization that, in both cases, they had begun with a woman named Helen.

After Ilium

CHAPTER 2

When he awoke on the first morning of the cruise, Alex Parris had looked out the porthole, which sat just above the waterline. He immediately had visions of the oars of the Achaeans' boats plying across the blue waters toward the shores of Asia Minor. The war was beginning. All for a woman.

Was it worth it? He had pondered that question on a bright, golden morning when he set out from Piraeus aboard the gleaming white cruise ship, *Aegean Princess.*

Alex loved to play historian. Anyone who asked him about it knew he really did mean *play*. He seemed to spend all his spare time since the early days of middle school gleefully acting out historical scenarios. He role-played generals and emperors, warriors and statesmen. He built castles in the basement, with towers, ramparts, drawbridges, and moats drawn in blue. As a boy, he had loved playing Hercules with the other children on his street, each day assigning them various roles, such as Hercules' matron, Hera, or even Zeus. He made Billy, the boy next door, play the many-headed Hydra one particular week by taping toy lizard heads to the skinny boy's shoulders.

His science projects focused on works of ancient engineering, a full range of artful contraptions he'd carefully manufactured from hardware store supplies and his own meticulously sketched designs. For several years, Alex had a huge diorama set up on a wide plywood sheet atop sawhorses in the basement, much the same way other boys erected elaborate train sets. It had begun as a more modest project. After perfecting the Waterloo battlefield he had created, he determined that he wouldn't be able to persuade his parents to purchase the vast numbers of toy soldiers to populate his diorama. So Alex had switched to the siege of Troy.

He knew the story well, although it wasn't until years later that he learned how the names came to be confused. A king named Dardanus had two sons, Tros and Ilus, and each founded a village in that northwest corner of Asia Minor. After several generations, the towns grew together and became one; people called it either Troy or Ilium, as they liked. The famous shining stone walls and "topless towers" of the great city, covered for centuries, Alex had constructed of plain cardboard. It was rather inauthentic, a squarish shape that followed Crusader castle design rather than Assyrian. The warriors on both sides were cast lead, and Alex had painted each of them in detail. He placed them among plastic trees, green foam bushes, and terrain made of real sand, pebbles, and red dirt. His father had taken a photograph of the Troy diorama, and a reporter from the community newspaper came out to interview Alex. He was thirteen.

The framed photograph of the diorama hung on a wall in his father's dentistry office for several years, long after Alex had become embarrassed at the amateurish nature of his creation. He had since moved on to video games, constructing urban simulations in digital graphics. The only aspect he disliked was that the simulation games were modern, not set in ancient or older historic times when everything was much more interesting.

It was good practice, he told his parents, for his career designing cities. They were very proud of him, pleased that he was interested in architecture. They seldom worried about the hours he spent at his computer. He always got good grades, remained clean-cut, polite, ambitious, and they couldn't imagine him ever trying illegal drugs or accepting an alcoholic beverage. They only searched his room once in a while—whenever there was a report on television about teens in trouble. He was never in trouble, of course. He was the perfect son, their only child.

So much was expected of him, Alex contemplated as he leaned against the railing of the upper deck, scanning the ship below. The brilliant noontide made him squint. That helped him shift into his notorious historical trance, a quiet place where he could relax for several minutes before returning to the mundane present.

If they had known it would be a ten-year siege, Alex thought, would they have gone? He was stuck again in one of his thought-puzzles as he watched the blue sea unzipping for the ship. If they had known that their greatest heroes would fall, that in the end they would only get a trunk full of treasure and a few leftover women of the walled city to sell as slaves or keep as concubines, would they have let Paris, the pimply-faced youth, keep his mature, beautiful Helen? Was it all worth such a war?

Alex thought of the woman he had seen upon boarding. She seemed to be a perfect model of Classical Helen. Actually, he admitted, she was a bit too curvy compared to how the famous Helen would have been. Helen of Troy would have been slender. Unless, of course, as a queen, she had so much leisure time that she put on weight.

Even so, he had to get to know the woman, he decided, leaning over the railing. There was something about her that caught his eye, something that drew him to her, but he could not decide what it was. Of course, while traveling across Europe since his graduation, Alex had seen a lot of pretty girls—*hot babes*, his frat brothers would call them, or worse terms. The girls he saw in England were nicely naughty, and the French girls properly decadent, while the girls of Italy were quite lovely in a girl-next-door or farmer's daughter way.

This woman, however, was the only one he had seen in a month of travel who really intrigued him. She was nothing like those skinny co-eds his fraternity brothers liked. She was nothing like those airbrushed centerfolds or the poster models that covered the walls of the frat house—except for her large bust. She did have that in common with the pictures.

He had learned well from his fraternity brothers what kind of girls to pursue: the ones who would give in and put out. He learned which girls were the fun ones, which ones to avoid, which ones could be emotionally abused and then accept some lame apology before submitting to more abuse. He saw how his brothers operated. He saw those girls before and after being with his frat brothers, and he was torn between being just one of the guys and being the one who would defend those girls from the bad behavior of his brothers.

Alex wasn't like them. He tried to tell some of the young women that, half as apology and half come-on. His brothers gave all men a bad reputation and he hated that. Alex hated it so much that he allowed the girls he dated to take advantage of his good nature. He would buy them dinner, take them to a show, and then only kiss their cheek at the end of the evening. He could wait for the right time to claim his lover. Soon he had gotten a reputation, too. He was a gentleman. Alex was a safe guy, a brotherly confidant. Girls did not need to worry about being out with him. He was the kind of man they would eventually decide to marry—after they had spent enough time fooling around with the kind of men like his frat brothers.

He was working himself into an angry mood thinking about his college life. He told himself that college was over. Now he was in what they had all jokingly called the 'real world'—some strange place of unpleasantness that used to scare them. He was no longer subject to the influence of his frat brothers, he knew. Calming down, he reminded himself that he was on vacation. It was his time to let loose, to be free, to try new things.

Then he saw her again: the intriguing woman—the

woman of intrigue—*her*.

She was on the deck below him as he surveyed the ship. She, too, was leaning against the railing, staring out at the sea. Alex watched her intently. When she stepped away from the railing, he hurried to the stairwell, descended and searched for her. He found her finally on the opposite side of the ship, scanning the horizon, watching the sun setting over the hill-crested islands they were passing. The bronze sun hovered like a street lamp over the chalky-brown islands, the deep golden light melting over the sparse greenery. That scene, surrounded by the brilliant blue of the sea, propelled him back to ancient times. He wanted to reach out and grasp it. Instead, he turned and headed down to the lower deck, chasing his dream lady.

He arrived anxiously, breathing hard, and threw on his brakes. There she was again—closer to him than he expected when he dismounted the stairs. His approach was too quick, he decided, so he stopped short behind the bulwark, then strolled casually past her, admiring the view like everyone else. He went along the railing as far as he could before the next bulwark forced him to halt. He set himself there, leaning against the railing, striking the pose of someone who was regarding the sea, hoping for some esoteric revelation.

She must be doing the same thing, he thought after a few minutes.

Studying her from a short distance, he contemplated the line he would use. Considering what his fraternity brothers would probably say, he shook off one then another line, then another. This was a very new situation.

There were no lines to say. Now was the time for him to strike off on his own.

He stood up straight, smoothed his wrinkled shirt, and approached her, sliding his hand up the railing to where she leaned.

"Beautiful sunset, don't you think?" the new and improved Alex Parris spoke as he paused near where she rested.

Her belly pressed against the railing, her breasts resting on the top rail, her gaze turned seaward. The woman did not acknowledge his presence, continued staring out at the sea.

"I love this time of day," he said. He made his voice as plain as possible, not too loud, not too soft, and added a positive timbre to the last word, elongating the vowel a little longer than necessary. He waited. After a minute his heart started to beat again.

She watched the sunset another minute more, then took a deep breath, as though she needed the fresh air as some kind of treasured dessert.

"Yes...," she spoke—at precisely the moment as he was about to say something to fill the silence, probably something stupid, he considered. Her voice, in a single syllable, was like smoke from an after-sex cigarette, with three gray rings slowly evaporating into the clarity of the sea breeze. Alex seemed to melt a little.

He waited another minute, thinking of the right sentence. She did not move. He was afraid to speak, afraid of saying something dumb which would cause her to leave. He ran through the list of lines he had heard his frat brothers use but none seemed right for a woman who was obviously more mature than his usual date. The corner of his mouth moved, turned upward as he was amused that he was already calling this encounter a date.

It was not a date, of course. He was simply being polite. No harm in that, right?

"I'm Alex," he said, a little too quickly. He cleared his throat. "Alex Parris."

She half-turned her head to him. "Hello, Alex Parris."

"Nice to meet you," he said.

The pressure of his stomach pushing against his vocal chords cut short his breath. He didn't think his voice had sounded manly enough. He'd better say something else, this time in a strong voice, or she'd classify him as a wimp.

"Nice to meet anyone on this cruise," he spoke up. "I mean, anyone...who who is...who's suitable for a cruise...like like this one. By suitable, I mean.... I mean, that we're going to Istanbul. I mean, from Athens to Istanbul. You look like...like you belong on this this cruise." He took a desperate breath. "What I'm trying to say is that you look perfect for being on a pleasure cruise to Istanbul. While I, me being an American—well, I don't think I quite fit. Do I?"

He hoped she would say something—anything to allow him to relax. Instead, she only nodded and looked back out at the sea.

"Am I right?" he asked, hesitantly. Self-deprecating humor had always endeared him to girls in college.

"It is a beautiful sea," she spoke softly, like a breeze carrying the scent of some flowers, spicy yet sweet.

"Yes, it is very beautiful," he responded, also staring out

at the sunset waters. His heart stopped pounding in his ears. The hard part was over; she had responded to him. "It's a wine-dark sea. That's what Homer called the Aegean. I guess it depends on what wine we're drinking, huh?"

She turned sharply and regarded him. Something had changed in her face: a subtle shift of molecules that signaled a change in her heart. A new distraction. The flicker of a different mood crossed her face like the play of light and shadow upon the waves. She adjusted her pose against the railing. A sweep of her hand through her thick, raven hair as the wind caught it and tossed it across her face, providing cover for her stratagems.

"Yes, whatever we are drinking."

He smiled, feeling energized. "By the way, what's your name?"

She startled. "My name?"

Pursing her lips, she seemed to be caught by surprise, as though she had misplaced her passport and was standing at the border. She stared at him as though he were a customs official, then seemed to be amused by him.

"You may call me…mmm…Ellen," she said, then added a quick smile almost as an afterthought, as something she decided she should do to be polite.

"Ellen…." He contemplated the name, but it did not fit. "Ellen? I thought you would be Greek. You look Greek. You look…well, very beautiful, of course. No matter what your name is. Classic beauty. I mean is...."

Her glance stopped him. "Thank you, Alex Parris." She returned her gaze to the sea. "I also am called Elaine, if you must know."

"So you are Greek, aren't you? I thought so."

"How many people do you see in Athens who are Greek?"

"A lot. But on a cruise like this, it's mostly tourists. Not so many are Greeks."

She laughed, then seemed to catch her *faux pas* and resumed her stern persona as he talked about Athens: the hostel where he stayed and the two guys who tried to steal his backpack; the Russian girl he met at a street vendor and who toured the Parthenon with him, then asked for taxi fare back to her fancy hotel; the trips he made to the nearby McDonald's because he didn't like dining alone in any of the finer restaurants; the spider bite he got while sleeping the previous night.

"You must be having fun," she said in lieu of a laugh.

"The best is yet to come," he said. "You see, from Istanbul I'm going to see Ilium. You know, Troy. Ancient Troy—or what's left of it. That's my ultimate destination. If I have any time after that—and enough money—I'll go see the Pyramids before heading home."

"All summer you travel around?"

"Not all summer, but most of it. I have a new job waiting for me so I can't travel *all* summer. How about you?"

Instead of a reply, she turned to the sea as the breeze coaxed a dance from her hair. Perhaps her answers were there among the darkening waves, thought Alex. The sea hides many thoughts, many deeds, after all. He smiled at his profound thought. This afternoon would never be a secret. He was proud of himself, at least to some small degree, for talking with this beautiful woman, for standing up for himself, being his own man. His fraternity brothers would be impressed—not that he needed to impress any of those guys.

"I do not know where I am going," she spoke suddenly, as if she had just then decided on the best answer, "and yet…perhaps I shall come to know where I belong soon enough. Perhaps this journey will show me that place. Do you think so?"

"I do believe so." He showed her his white teeth so she would know he was sincere. "Anything is possible, Ellen."

"Ah! Don't call me Ellen," she almost snapped. "Too American."

"Then what should I call you?"

"My name is Eléna," she said, elongating the middle vowel brightly, like swinging open the shutters to let in the sunshine on a fresh spring morning.

"El*éééé*na," he whispered, trying hard to match her pronunciation.

"Do not play with my name, Alex Parris."

"Sorry. But that's better," he said with a chuckle. "That sounds Greek. Now I believe you. Now I know what attracted me to you." He stopped, recognizing how he was about to stumble into his old trap: falling in love too quickly, falling for any girl who was nice to him. The worst was when he let himself express his feelings to a woman before he knew how she felt about him. That always signaled a loser.

"But I am Greek," she said cheerfully. "Apollodorus is my family name."

"Apollodorus," Alex again whispered, testing his pronunciation.

"Good. You sound Greek, too."

"So you *are* Greek."

"Yes," she said hesitantly. She seemed to wink at him. "Now I'm from America."

Without warning, his eyes latched onto hers and for a heartbeat he could see into her soul. She blinked yet he was again able to look into her beautiful, dark eyes. He grabbed the railing for support, resisting the urge to stay locked with her eyes.

"So tell me your story, Eléna," he said, unsure where the words came from. A wave of nervousness ran through him. "I mean, how did you come to be on this cruise to Istanbul? On this tour across the Aegean? And did you realize that you and I are fated to be together? According to the gods, that is."

Eléna did not smile. "Is this what you always say when you meet someone on a cruise?"

"I don't know," he said, and a chuckle tumbled awkwardly from his mouth, "it's my first cruise."

They both laughed and their voices seemed to dance in the air between them—like lovers, thought Alex, like two fated soul mates who were just discovering that they had been matched by the gods and were about to set off on a journey of a lifetime, hand in hand, heart to heart—because she was Greek: as Greek as the Aegean was blue. He knew from all his studies of ancient Greece that *Eléna* was merely the Greek form of the name worn by the woman most people knew from history as Helen.

She spoke hesitantly, choosing her words carefully, separating what could be told from what must remain secret. He could respect that, not that he had any secrets worth hiding. As he listened, transfixed on the smoky tone of her voice, he noticed her accent was slightly British on some words while decidedly foreign on others. He liked her accent, so he tried to coax longer answers from her but she preferred to keep her words to herself. Her thoughts, too. That could have been enough for him, or any young man seriously away from home for the first time.

The silences she wove between her breaths made her even more exotic to him, and compellingly seductive—especially the way the breeze tugged at her long hair, so jet-black, so wavy, lush, and voluminous. He traced her perfect Classical profile with his eyes: the high forehead and short, straight nose, her pouty, full lips, the noble chin, and the slender, graceful throat where the sunlight seemed to cover any hint of middle age. He studied her closely: she was middle aged, he accepted. However, that did not make her any less beautiful. The way her thin, flower-patterned skirt twisted around her knees, backlit by the setting sun so that her profile was revealed, enticed him. Her petite toes, with their red-painted nails like drops of blood, peeped out of her sandals. The way her white cotton blouse fell open to the sea, visible to the curious gulls but not to him, urged him on.

She intrigued him as any beautiful woman would, however, knowing her name made all the difference in the world. Alex had to grin. He had stepped through Fate's door. He could not resist pointing out to Eléna the irony of their meeting: she being 'Helen' and he with the surname 'Parris'. It could not be mere coincidence, he insisted. Their meeting, he explained, was intended.

That made her turn and regard him, size him up.

"Fate?" she asked him, impatience in her voice.

Alex watched for signs of impending violence, then replied: "Well, yes. Fate. That's what people call it. The gods—I mean, the gods and goddesses in Greek mythology—they loved to play games with their favorite mortals. So whatever your god had in mind for you was your fate and you couldn't escape it."

"I have no personal gods or goddesses. I make my own fate."

"Then you believe in fate. Right?"

"I believe I have the power to change my destiny."

"Destiny…that's another story."

"You are full of stories, yes?" She almost laughed, or wanted to laugh yet held it back, something she did not want him to see.

"We are all stories," he responded, then waited to catch her response. Nothing. His words hung in the air. "Whatever we do and say, who we meet and…and fall in love with…who we make families with…and work hard to support, to protect. That's our story." He felt a bit taller, stronger now. The gods were filling him with confidence. The muse was favoring him tonight. "Life is a story. I mean, each of our lives becomes a story in itself. In fact, my Philosophy professor, Doctor Kammerer, said that if we look at the events we—"

"Why are you taking this voyage? Is it your fate?" A

smile crept onto her face briefly before she sent it away. "Do you expect to test your gods?"

Alex chuckled, to show he had a sense of humor. His smile displayed his pearly teeth and the glint caught her eye, he could tell, yet her face remained artificially grim.

"No, I've finally finished all my tests," he said proudly. "Now I'm free to see the treasures of antiquity and the battlefields of history."

"There is always one more test," said Eléna in a voice full of bad dreams.

Alex was silent, staring at her body, at her beauty, in amazement, recalling the dream from long ago when he was told the answers to the test by a bearded, robed wiseman, then scored perfect the next day. He did not have many dreams of women, yet he did often daydream.

She returned to her examination of the seascape.

"I guess so," he said, finally.

Alex thought he had set the right balance of sincerity and sophistication. He was non-threatening yet inviting. Maybe he had said something offensive. Still, she did not move away. She leaned against the railing, obviously not feeling threatened by him being there. He should have expected that. He was as innocent as one of the potted plants that lined the deck. Or the complimentary towels at the swimming pool. Part of the ship. He could see that clearly.

Alex focused on that one fact: she did not leave.

As he spoke in soft, even tone about the sites he had seen in Athens, she seemed to take an interest in him, tolerating his presence beside her.

"And, of course, the Acropolis, the very foundation of Democracy, is everyone's first stop, most definitely," he explained, "and it's really the start of geometry, too. The Parthenon is a veritable textbook of architecture. So that's required. I spent the whole day there, sketching it. I have to show you my drawings. I used to study Architecture, then switched to History. Classical columns always fascinate me—the different styles of scrolls, especially. And then I walked around the Plaka each night. Couldn't decide what to eat or what to buy. I have to travel light, so no souvenirs for me. Unless it's something special. And yesterday I went on the half-day trip out to Cape Sounion, you know, where the Temple of Poseidon is. Great architecture. Where I'm from—California—nothing is old, or maybe a hundred years, at best. It's the ancient things I like. You know, one of the best things I visited was the Agora. People at the hostel said to skip it but I went there anyway. The Temple of Hephaestus is there—as you probably know—with a pretty good museum and a lot of monuments. You touch one of those stones and you can feel the thousands of years of history there in the dust." He took a long breath, as though he were reliving the moment. "I just sat there for a long time, looking out at the world, thinking about my future, stuff like that. Fantastic place."

"I have not seen it," said Eléna. "Perhaps on my way back home."

"You should see it. I also went to that Syntagma Square—a great plaza but too crowded for me. Too many 'real' tourists there, the four-star hotel kind of tourists—

the kind who never really see anything, never want to see what is real, never want to get a feel for the place they're at. They don't want to touch the rocks and imagine another time and place. They only care about now. They want everything in the new place to be like it was in the place they left. I have to get out and walk the streets, bump shoulders with people, get dirty, breathe the smells, step in shit, trip and fall, maybe get in a fight. Then I've really experienced a place. I don't want a neat little postcard tour."

He had stepped closer, to within arm's length, as he talked. Now he leaned against the railing beside her. He continued telling her about his three days in Athens, as though he were giving a report at school. As he did, he kept an eye on the woman beside him. He was not boring, he was glad to know. After all, she did not leave.

When he finally paused, she glanced at him, perhaps wondering if he had run out of things to say. His throat was dry by then. He thought of inviting her to have a drink with him.

"Eléna, would you…?" He hesitated.

They were both staring out at the sea. Alex could not read her thoughts, could not sense her disposition. His own mind was going crazy, his heart beating faster. The sky was darker, the sea black beneath the moonlight, and he knew he was running out of time. Tomorrow was another lifetime.

"Would you like to g—"

"I can tell you are trying hard," she said suddenly, at the precise moment when he nudged a bit closer, perhaps too close.

He started to speak, stopped. His hands grasped the railing.

"What do you mean?" he asked.

She smiled—to be polite, it seemed to Alex.

"I am complimenting you."

"For what?" he asked. He scratched at his furrowed brow.

"Your...flirtations. Let's call it that. You have practiced them, yes?" She waited, still smiling, then recognized that he did not understand. "You have been very kind, Alex Parris. Thank you for the distraction."

He nodded quickly, in thanks for a compliment or in acceptance of his well-known flaws. He couldn't decide.

"Distraction?" he asked, almost a whisper.

"It is going to be a lovely evening," she said, changing her pose.

They remained against the railing of the cruise ship, gazing out at the once crystalline sea, now fading in the dusk. He stared at her and soon realized she knew he was staring at her yet let him proceed. She liked him watching her, he decided. What was she watching? Not him. He had flashed his white smile often enough, and he was physically fit and a gentleman, too. And he had flirted with her. No, thought Alex, it was not about him. She seemed to be searching for something. He could sense it. The distraction was hers. The way she gazed out at the sea so absently, deep in thought, and the way she always held herself, arms wrapped around her torso as though no-one else would.

He continued to give her his impressions of the Greek historical sites and his plans for touring Istanbul when they arrived. Eléna was listening; she tilted her head his direction. She asked him more questions about Athens, about one museum in particular he had visited: the National Archaeological Museum, which held artifacts from the ancient eras of Greek history. The museum's statue of a smiling Aphrodite preparing to slap a satyr with her sandal was his favorite, and the huge *kouros* statues with their enigmatic smiles, the clean, clear lines of early Cycladic artifacts, and the large, rich gold masks and ornaments from Mycenae left him eager for Ilium. He enjoyed describing all of it to her and she returned the good cheer to him with an occasional grin.

They were having a conversation. He could not keep his eyes from caressing her figure, down to her toes and up to her eyes, slowly and surreptitiously embracing her in his mind. His hands itched to hold her, to squeeze her body. As he stared at her crisp, white blouse, he saw that the upper button was now unbuttoned. When the breeze caught her blouse, he could see the lacey edge of her bra.

He was close enough now that her arm accidentally brushed his as she shifted against the railing. She did not react to the touch; he imagined she did it purposefully. She was testing him, he thought. Maybe, at the ripe age of twenty-two, his time for corruption had come.

"I am impressed that you try to impress me," Eléna told him, and turned to rest her back against the railing, presenting her voluptuous figure to him. "You should give yourself points for trying, then be satisfied and leave."

Alex thought he detected a subtle, teasing sense of humor beneath her words, and he could feel her stern resolve beginning to melt. She couldn't really be asking him to leave, could she? Not after they had been talking for so long—for what? more than an hour? She cared about his obvious attempts to get to know her.

He pointed to the rugged island they were passing, soon to be lost in the dusk, remarking casually on the wild landscape but thinking of her: rocky mountains opening to a fertile vale. She gazed out at the scene and replied as if he were some kind of statue, a mute but attentive listener. Alex was content to let her voice flow over him, no matter what she was saying. The accent falling from her mouth tickled his ears—just as her tongue would lick his ear lobes—

He broke from his trance.

"That's very interesting," he said automatically.

This woman, was obviously older than he was, was alone on an Aegean cruise. She had to be thirty-five, he decided, maybe older. Yet she had not given him the excuse that she was with someone. A woman her age did not travel alone. She had to be part of a couple, or a family, or at least in a tour group. If she really were alone, then she was beginning to accept him. She might welcome him as her traveling companion. Alex knew he could be charming, but now he was having difficulty imagining what his next move was going to be. He had never expected to get this far. Then he cursed himself: *this far?* He had been further than this with Suzie Meyer. This was no different, he told himself.

He breathed in her musky-sweet Greek aura. She accepted his presence, seemed to enjoy his company, but was this conversation all he would achieve on this cruise? Alex wanted to kick himself. It was a moment when the gentleman should offer the lady a cigarette—if this were *cinema verité*. But he did not smoke, had no lighter, and he was nervous enough already.

"I'm sorry," he said suddenly, fatally sincere.

Eléna cracked a smile.

"Sorry? Why?" she said, teasing. "Have you slipped once more over the line between common courtesy and rudeness?"

He instinctively glanced down at the deck, imagined the cracks between the boards as a boundary line. He was invading her space. Yet he refused to back away.

"I don't think so," he said, standing straight.

"I am sure you're a nice boy," she spoke, as though she were pausing to puff on her imaginary cigarette. "You must by now see I am too old for you."

Boy? Too old? What had he missed seeing from the time he first watched her saunter up the gangway? All the moments since then, when her gaze hovered over the railing as if longing for distant shores even before they had set off from the port of Piraeus? The mystery that shadowed her continued to seduce him.

Right then, he wanted to tell her how beautiful he thought she was, to capture her attention once more, to make her know he was serious. He didn't think he could say it without sounding stupid. He also wanted to see her nude, maybe photograph her—as art, he would say. He had never so much as set foot in an art studio, yet he believed his talent would rise quickly once he was properly inspired by someone with a figure like hers.

What would come next was obvious to him, but he shuddered at the thought of actually getting his wish. He wanted to *lay* with her—to use the archaic expression he preferred. He was, after all, an out-of-fashion romantic. Yet that was a long way off, he knew. When he mentioned how her special, historic name had set him off, he saw how her expression soured.

It would take time; he would have to work up to it.

Fortunately, there were four days more before they reached Istanbul. The ship was scheduled to dock at ports around the Aegean so tourists could see all the sites and spend all their money.

So he planned to pursue her each day. He stepped painstakingly across ragged and rocky Crete, and caught her when she slipped on a loose rock. He also pursued her almost all the way through the ruins of the ancient Minoan city of Knossos, the tour guide droning on and on without any enthusiasm. Next day, he went, rather proudly, cheerfully with her down to royal Rhodes, feeling like a triumphant conqueror with saucy barbarian queen in tow. Slowly and patiently, like a dentist working a root canal, he maneuvered around Mykonos with her, taking her hand to help her up a hillside, letting her pat his back, dutifully bringing the lunch boxes to their table. Then, with excitement at the possibilities, he hurriedly climbed over the ever-intriguing and always mysterious Delos, where she called him by name, where she gave him the time of day. It was there that her eyes had smoldered for him, her body aching for his hands to pleasure her. That is what he imagined. Each night he could only lie in his stateroom and masturbate furiously.

The next day, the cruise ship sailed past the gently rounded, bosomy hills of Lésvos and that evening Alex imagined caressing her breasts, pictured how they would overfill his cupped hands, her nipples like ripe cherries waiting to be plucked. He'd always liked that metaphor. He lay back on his shipboard bunk, holding her image in his mind: dreaming of her breasts, and the hot, shadowy crevasse below, where the fountain of youth flowed. Then he would be pushing roughly into her, like Achaeans' ships bearing warriors, charging boldly, fiercely up through the narrow, gushing Dardanelles—just as their cruise ship would do in a couple more days.

He sighed after every night's climax, feeling ashamed.

CHAPTER 3

They arrived with little celebration on the banks of the wide Bosporus to begin their tour of exotic Istanbul.

In their five-day cruise, Alex didn't think he had managed to wear Eléna down much, but she at least no longer waved him off in the dining room. They had shared a laugh or two during the island tours, and their eyes had met across the decks of the ship, the rocky island paths, even in the bare terra cotta ruins of the Palace of Minos. He knew there was something happening between them, something that was making them grow closer. Indeed, after visiting Lésvos, she waved him to her table; she needed someone to amuse her as she dined. He guessed she saw him as easy-going, someone she could dine with who was non-threatening. Of course, he would never be rude intentionally, and he certainly would never get abusive with a woman like some of his fraternity brothers had done. He was raised to be a gentleman, a romantic gentleman.

She had come up to the railing beside him to watch the blood-and-gold sunset as they crossed the Sea of Marmara.

That was a good sign, he thought, feeling an erection coming on. Their elbows bumped and he felt a flash of excitement run through him.

One thing bothered him, though, enough to make him lose his concentration that night in his stateroom. Eléna seldom smiled, and when she did, she always seemed to cover her smile with a hand or let her scarf be blown there by the wind. Alex could picture her eyes in his dreams, and certainly her voluptuous figure, but her smile remained a mystery. He learned from his father, the orthodontist, that a person's moral character could be easily determined by the state of the person's teeth. So Alex had tried to spy her teeth at every opportunity but could never see them clearly. His brilliant, white smile, of course, matched perfectly the sweet, innocent boy his parents had raised.

Yes, he knew she had secrets, but uncovering them was not as great a priority as satisfying his quota of youthful indiscretions.

Alex checked his smile in a galley window, frowned briefly—he wish he had time to brush again—then went to the deck and sidled up to Eléna at their usual railing to watch the ship's docking procedures. She turned to regard him with a lustful gaze as strong as those he saw in his dreams of her. His perfect smile was powerless in the dim light of their evening arrival at Istanbul. Suddenly, Alex felt defenseless, unarmed. He was ripe for corruption as Eléna's full lips brushed his freshly shaved cheek, leaving a feathery tickle which haunted him as he returned to his room to gather his bags for disembarking. He could feel her lips on his cheek all through his brushing and flossing routine, and the thought of her lips on his made his body quiver.

In the parking area beside the wharf waited the tour bus that would take them to their hotel. Climbing aboard, Alex saw that Eléna had saved the seat beside her for him. She gave the cushion a little pat with her hand.

ꙮ

"What are you looking for?" Alex asked Eléna between tips of the tall wine bottle in her hotel room overlooking the Golden Horn.

She gently rubbed the edge of her glass with her fingertip, feeling its flesh catch on the crystal. Reclined on the neatly made-up bed, she gazed at him from under her bundle of hair. He was waiting for her answer, taking pleasure in winning her heart, patiently, like a gentlemanly seducer.

"Do I seem like a woman in search of something?" she responded at last.

"Yes. Unless you are just bored. Is that it?"

"Yes, I am very bored," she responded casually. She rolled onto her belly, looking at him sitting in a chair beside the bed. Her lips parted and her breath was heavy, her voice full of the bitterness of stuffed grape leaves and the spice of the *souvlaki* they had for dinner.

"I can see you are," said Alex. He knew what was going to happen next, but he was suddenly hesitant. He got up and sat on the edge of the bed, ready for anything.

Eléna, seeing his dismay, withdrew her invitation. She

had kicked off her sandals and now dug her toes into the bedspread. He gazed at them. Her toes were tiny, plump buttons that seemed afterthoughts to her delicately shaped feet. They held his attention perhaps a moment too long. He studied her smooth, rounded heels, then focused on her red-painted toenails. Like drops of blood, he thought.

He slowly stretched his hand toward her foot.

"And what are you looking for, Alex Parris?" she asked, a dark, misty distance in her voice. She took another sip of wine. "An adventure in a foreign land, perhaps? You are newly away from your home, yes? Is that why you come on this journey?"

Alex regarded her. His hand froze.

"Partly." Suddenly he felt thirteen again, interrogated by his parents after hanging out with some of his 'questionable' friends. His throat was tight. He swallowed hard. "Mostly I just wanted to see these ancient places. Battlefields, mostly. Historic buildings, too. Castles and palaces. Museums. Ruins of famous places. That's what I studied in college. History, I mean. Lots of history, especially European history, and its origins in Middle Eastern history. I told you my specialty is ancient history, particularly Greece and Rome." His eyes slipped back to her red toenails as they moved slowly back and forth across the bedspread. Her ankles seemed a little too aggressive, her calves dangerously curved, her knees something sacred. "I majored in History, I mean. I mean, that was my degree. History—"

"Come, look in my eyes."

She pulled herself up onto her bent elbow.

Alex leaned toward her, feeling off-balance as the soft surface of the bed shifted. As he struggled to hold his eyes on hers, his attention was drawn away in alternate heartbeats to Eléna's bosom. Her blouse lay open just beneath his gaze. His breathing quickened.

She sensed where his attention was and lifted her hand, released another button on her blouse. Her white, lacey bra was exposed. She was offering herself to him. Or was she only teasing?

"I'm looking," he said. "In your eyes, I mean."

"No, you are not."

His heart was beating fast and he felt it in his ears.

"I'm sorry." That was all he could think of to say. Alex felt the scolding glare of his mother. He had been raised to be a gentleman, after all. "I didn't mean to, umm, stare."

"Do not worry," she whispered, "I forgive you."

"I only asked you what you're looking for, Eléna," he spoke in a stronger voice, relieved at the chance to clear the air. He wanted to go ahead but he was afraid. "It's a rhetorical question. You know, a conversation starter."

She studied him a moment, then rolled onto her back, caressing the bedspread.

"Do you wish to have conversation now?"

He swallowed hard again, his heart pounding. "No...."

"Let me show you what I search for, since you are so curious."

Eléna stretched casually across the bed, against him, her shoulder touching his chest, and turned her head back to gaze upon his face. Her hand took his free hand and carried it along the length of her belly. He stiffened as she escorted his fingers down between her thighs. At the same time, she stretched up and brushed his cheek with her lips. When he turned to meet her eyes, she took his face in one hand and drew his mouth to hers.

"Me?" he asked. "You're looking for me?"

"Not exactly." She kissed his mouth. Parting, she looked him over. "Yet you will do."

As her mouth began to close, Alex rushed to kiss her, wrapping his arms awkwardly around her. Measured by his arm, her waist was not skinny, but her supple flesh still soothed him. It was a nurturing flesh; it gave way and welcomed him. His other hand felt the heaviness of her breasts. Eléna took his hands in hers and pulled them up her belly to her breasts. She encircled him with her arms. They rolled backwards on the bed, she on top of him. He rolled them over again, expecting he would be on top, where he would be more comfortable. Instead, they spilled over the edge of the bed and landed hard on the floor next to the wall, Alex on the bottom.

Clumsy idiot, he cursed himself. However, he found her already prying open his shirt. She was oblivious to the popping buttons flying across the carpet. He could afford a new shirt, he decided, feeling the light touch of Eléna's fingers coursing over his thinly muscled chest and circling around his nipples.

She lay against him, her bra-cupped breasts to his bare chest, and he was aroused and about to lose control.

Eléna reached back and unhooked her bra, allowing the fullness of her breasts to fill his face. She lowered herself, pressing her hips against his, grinding against his erection with increasing impatience.

"Are you afraid?" she whispered into his ear.

"No," Alex muttered, trying to gain confidence. His voice was shaking, however.

He fought to kick his parents out of his head as he swelled with lust at Eléna's rough touch, at the practiced manner in which her fingers released his desire, at the way her soft lips teased him and goaded him deeper into the night.

Finally, he was getting what he deserved, what his fraternity brothers had always taken so freely. See a girl, take a girl—and he was left to clean up their mess, literally and figuratively. Alex, the good guy, the shoulder to cry on when they got dumped, the sweet boy who would never hurt them. Now it was his turn. He was going to take all that he could.

However, his parents had tricked him, had made him feel guilty for the slightest naughty thought, for showing the slightest desire. He could not relax.

I'm not a kid any longer. I graduated. I'm a man now. This is my reward. This is my time, Mother and Dad. Leave me alone!

"Shhhh," Eléna whispered. She pulled him back onto the bed. "Let me enjoy you."

He imagined that he was about to go sailing on a wild, stormy ocean. No telling what would happen! He expelled a big breath, freeing his anxiety, and the woman knew it was time to raise the anchor.

She guided him on a tour of her body, and he was

willing to explore each port of entry, languishing there until she called him to continue sailing her fragrant seas. She invited him to climb her sacred hills and navigate himself into position so she could entertain him with all of the sweet delights from her bag of tricks. He found there a treasure trove of new sensations being forced upon him. She coaxed him onward with sweet whispered words and dainty nibbles, and they felt the bed shaking, much like the swaying of the ship—just as ancient Helen and Paris must have felt as the two of them set sail for Troy, he considered—now rocking them into a sacred rhythm. Her fingers raked his back and shoulders as he willingly stretched then confidently pushed and forcefully strained and with enraged power released the iron gate to the gushing flood of life: all the books, all the classes, all the exams, all the rules of his parents and the stupidity of his fraternity brothers, and the church and the importance of perfect teeth and the essays for scholarships, and all the strict years and months and weeks of frustration and being a *good little boy!*—launching all at once into the deep, deep well of memories, lost forever in a swirling instant of naked, humbling ecstasy. She waited, shaking, until the memory had evaporated and he breathed once more, feeling the tension in his body flee in terror.

He continued collecting souvenirs as she directed him southward, showing him a lush garden of delicious, juicy fruit to sample, even daring him to taste the puckered kumquat. The festive banquet of Eden spread before him! Drowning in the sea of pleasure, she sighed, like the wind in the sails, and encouraged him to gather all the treasures that he could. He responded by lapping furiously at the fountain of youth, growing not younger but older, gaining maturity. And when he feared he might finally be satiated, she called for him to return to port, to push hard into the harbor until his vessel was fully docked and his wares completely unloaded.

Feeling more adventurous, her captain elected to set sail again, to journey once more over the now-charted seas, revisiting his favorite isles, until he again returned to homeport and unloaded the jewels she had for so long awaited.

In the end, she was satisfied far more than she had expected to be, and much more than she had been for many years of married life. He listened to her confession as though it were a siren's song. She had nearly forgotten how wonderful such a vacation trip could possibly be. She kissed her loving captain for what seemed endless days and weeks, and thanked him sincerely for the voyage. And he, spiritually exhausted and morally bankrupt beyond reason, reluctantly surrendered into her gentle hands his last ounce of gold.

By then, not knowing the hour of the night, Alex lay as still as a corpse, with Eléna brushing her breasts across his face, collecting kisses, and he could no longer recall his parents, nor did he believe he had ever been born.

CHAPTER 4

When dawn crept into their room, Alex believed he now understood her life. Eléna was not a woman alone on a cruise as he had first suspected. She never cruised alone, she had revealed in recesses from their lovemaking. He did not get her humor. For Eléna, there was only the husband occupied with his career, the long idle hours at home, the two children who demanded her attention, especially when their nanny was off for the day, and what Alex translated in his mind as the endless days full of despair. He insisted he understood what she meant when she spoke of the light that had once shone at the end of the tunnel growing dim for her, the years lying down like dominoes and dying away before her eyes. This she had to flee, Alex realized. To run away and find herself—or find someone who also was running away.

He was so much like her, he decided—at least in the ways that mattered to them. They were both seeking new directions: away from the old routines that had threatened to suck away their souls, to something vastly different, something desirable.

They lay together in the large bath basin in her room, embraced in the hot, scented water, among the luxuriant suds. Sitting in the space between his legs and resting her back against his chest, she spoke freely, pleasantly in her soft, dark voice, about their travels to the islands of the Aegean. Alex held her in his arms, listening. He was taking the role of confidant again that he was all too used to when in the company of college girls. This, however, was not the same. He wished his frat brothers could see him now. Alex Parris had grown up—and he had a grown-up woman to prove it.

Eléna felt at ease. She tilted her head, hair tied to the side, against his throat.

"Are you comfortable here?" Alex checked.

"Yes, very comfortable."

Yet it had not always been so, as he heard.

Eléna had left her husband, an older man set in his world of high finance who filled an expensive home in the countryside with all that he could afford for her, and for the two children who inevitably came later. She had to leave. Alex saw her situation as living in a gilded cage, though he did not share the idea with her. He considered that he lived in a similar gilded cage: the nice suburban home his father had worked hard to provide, his doting mother, the ex-kindergarten teacher. His parents' every effort was aimed at providing him with comfort and a carefree existence. It was a simple deal: he was only required to make them proud. A spasm of anger rippled through him at that thought.

Eléna was startled and turned back to kiss him.

"Relax, Alex Parris. What could you have to worry you?"

He smiled quickly.

She stood, soapy water running down her body, and reversed her position, facing him. Once seated again, she took his face in her hands and kissed him. Feeling the tension in him, she brought her hand up to his chest, caressing him with her gently clawing fingertips. Her fingers pushed against his skin.

"Your body is…tight," she remarked, reaching around to scratch his back.

"I try to work out," he said. "The frat house had all kinds of equipment in it, but I—"

"Shhhh." She put her finger against his mouth. "The time for talking is done. Now let us feel. Talk with your hands. Listen with your heart."

Alex listened with his heart, and felt everything. For Eléna, adulthood had come upon her too quickly. Or so Alex believed from her soft-spoken laments. He started to get the idea that it was the same for him. Of course, the words Eléna used were a very different, more flowery language, some of it Greek when she let her emotions flow. He was in the adult world now so her language—too much about daycare, mortgages, garden parties, country clubs, charity benefits—compelled him to decipher it in order to understand her. He knew what he needed to know. At thirty-eight, she now sought another round of flagrant youth, another chance to be carefree—simply to be free.

Alex pondered what he would be like at that age, with those responsibilities, those problems. He considered whether or not he would also run away from them, as she had done. He did not want to think about that now.

After drying off, Eléna donned her robe, leaving Alex to lounge in a towel wrapped around his hips. They ordered room service. The elegant, wheeled tray was presented to 'Mr. and Mrs. Smith', and Alex did not correct the waiter.

Maybe Alex was ready for his newfound freedom, after all. Eléna, robe pulled around herself, leaned down and gently kissed his forehead as he gazed up at her from the edge of the bed. Domestic tranquility. Alex sighed and began devouring the meal set before him.

"My aunt and uncle, Nena and Gregór, they told me to watch out for myself in Turkey," said Eléna, sitting beside him as they ate their breakfast. She whispered something Greek in his ear with a giggle, and then nibbled his lobe. "Being Greek, of course they would hate all things Turkish. We are still much alike, yet they see none of that. They do not want me to travel alone. They don't want me to set foot in Turkey at all."

"That's understandable," Alex mumbled, chewing the spinach crêpes. "And here you are traveling alone, after all."

"Of course, they do not have a clue why I dropped in so unexpectedly," Eléna continued, ignoring him. "I speak English at them and they just nod their heads like they understand me. If I spoke Greek, I would have to be honest. In English I can lie." She threw back her head and laughed, full throated, and Alex was caught off-guard. She was excited to be confessing to him: "I practically burst into their house in Athens—like a thunderstorm! They hurried to make up a room for me. They did not know what to do, so old-fashioned they are. Silly people! We Greeks, Alex Parris—those of us born in Greece—we do these things. We are spontaneous, bold—and for a woman, fiery. You must understand this if we are to continue."

Alex walked his hand up her thigh, something he had seen in a movie, and she feigned a slap to his hand but allowed it to remain.

"I understand *this*," he said, letting a slight chuckle slip out. "Let's continue."

If it was to be only a one-night stand, he could be satisfied with that. He sensed more was possible. He wanted more.

Maybe it was the sex, maybe the wine, he thought, but he doubted it was either. Maybe it was his willingness to allow her to feel comfortable, to accept her confessions. For once, he was in the right place at the right time. He was the kind of man she needed last night, he considered, feeling a tinge of pride. They were connecting on another level. A relationship was growing out of their sexual union.

"We must go on the tour," she said with equal parts regret and excitement.

"I want to tour you, Helen." He was confident now, and ready to take risks.

"My name is *Eléna*."

"Sorry," he mugged. "Helen, Eléna, or simply Elaine, it doesn't matter to me."

"No?" She popped up, stern-faced, and went to her suitcase. "I am not your mythic princess, Alex Parris!"

She dug through her clothing, searching for the day's outfit. She selected a folded dress, then a bra and panty, and set them on the bed.

"I know that," he admitted, still in a playful mood. "I was just imagining."

"Imagining?" She spun around, glaring at him. "I believed you were making love to *me* last night, not some ghost. Were we not in the same bed? Were you not inside me? Did you not enjoy our fucking? How dare you insult me that way!"

Alex was stunned. Obviously, he still needed to keep his guard up.

"That's not what I meant," Alex backpedaled. "You're so gorgeous I couldn't imagine making love with anyone else. I *didn't* imagine anyone else. You're all I've thought about since I first saw you on the ship, my love." Alex did not intend to add the affectionate tag. It just came out. She did nothing to acknowledge it, so he considered himself lucky and continued. "I was only thinking that, well, you know, you're so perfect for the part. I intended it as a compliment. I mean, if I were casting for a Hollywood film, I would choose you in a second for Helen of Troy. It is fate meeting you like this. I majored in History, Eléna, so it's never completely out of my mind. I tend to see things as they were, not as they are. I hear echoes from the past—like the whole Helen and Paris story. You, me, we fit the parts so perfectly. They believed in fate back then. It's no different from us meeting like this. It's fate, too."

"Again with your fate!"

Alex caught her facial expression in the mirror and she turned away. She was brushing her long black mane, pretending to ignore him.

"You're Greek and you don't believe in fate?" Alex was amazed, but she did not respond. "Eléna, when you see it, you'll understand. Then you'll see how you and I are meant to be together. Just like the ancient Helen and Paris."

"When you are young, you can afford to believe in fate. Later, you see how weak and foolish your belief was," Eléna lectured him. She stopped combing out her long hair and waved the comb like a sword at him. "You see how many accidents, how many mistakes you were willing to call fate. Then you understand there is no fate."

"But there has to be," Alex insisted. "I met *you*. Here. Just like Helen and Paris. On the way to Ilium. It can't be just a coincidence."

She stepped away from the mirror, grabbing the bra and panties from the bed.

"It may be luck, or fortune, for you, in meeting me. Only today and tomorrow will tell us," said Eléna, slipping off the robe, standing full-bodied and nude before him. Alex looked away, trying to be polite, then slowly returned his eyes to her. "Yet that is not the same as the kind of fate you foolishly seek. That kind is nothing but a fantasy."

She put on her underwear, then seemed ready to cry. Alex jumped up from the bed, his towel almost coming loose. Rather than needing comfort, however, he found her quite composed. He wanted to take it back. He didn't want to let her know how easily he would react at her slightest whim.

"Fate, Alex Parris, is when you die *exactly* when and how you wish it," she said in a flat, even tone, and stepped into the bathroom. She began applying her cosmetics.

Alex was puzzled. He dared not question her further, afraid of antagonizing her more.

He noticed then, in his exuberance, that his towel had fallen to the floor. Observing her transformation before the bathroom mirror, he did not bother to retrieve the towel and cover himself. He stood naked behind her, facing her in his mirrored image. When she finished her make-up, she returned to the bed and slipped into a bright, flower-patterned dress with spaghetti straps. She reached behind and tied the strings in a bow below her shoulder blades; she needed no help from him.

He sat uninhibitedly on the foot of the bed, watching her intently, content to bask in her aura as she set her foot on the bed and rubbed lotion up and down her leg. The only sounds he heard were the friction of her hands on her thighs and the shuffling of the hem of her dress. He was becoming concerned that she had not yet spoken.

Finally, he *felt* naked in the unanswered silence.

"What did you mean by what you said?" asked Alex.

She stood and grabbed his pants from the chair by the door, tossed them to him, a forceful motion that made him uneasy. Alex shyly pulled them on. His room was downstairs with its still unused bed, still holding his backpack full of clothing.

She followed him down the corridor.

"You're Greek. You should know the story," said Alex, deciding to press the issue when they entered his room. "I'm not trying to beat you over the head with it, Eléna, but you have to admit it's sort of spooky the way you and I match ancient history so well. I'm not trying to make up something, you know. Think about it. What if your name was Josephine and mine was Napoleon and we just happened to meet in Paris? We would be meant for each other. It's fate, like I said."

"I never believe in such coincidences as those," Eléna responded sternly, sitting on his bed, waiting for him to change his clothes. "There is no fate for us, Alex Parris. I told you about my husband. And my children."

"Your husband...and children?"

Eléna clapped her hands. "Hah! You were so into your sexual high jinks you have already forgotten me telling you about them. Now you know about them. Again."

"High jinks?" He pouted. "I thought we were pretty good together. We had this great kind of...what's it called? *Synergy*. Like we were in a cool kinda rhythm. I felt it. Didn't you? I mean, we were just...*wow*!"

He reached for her, thinking an embrace was called for at that moment.

"Wow? I've never heard it described so beautifully." She crossed her arms over her chest and let out a weary sigh. Alex took it to mean she might be finished with him already. "Yes, Alex Parris, you were good. You made me feel good. You have a wonderful natural ability. Call it instinct. It makes up for your...inexperience."

"Inexperience?" Alex placed his hands roughly on his hips. "I've been with women before. Well, college girls. That wasn't my first time, Eléna."

She glared at him, a look which reminded him of his mother when he did something inappropriate.

"Yes, it was."

He started to object, then thought better of it. What did it matter now? Besides, the limited experience he'd had was nothing to boast about. Suzie Meyer was nothing like the night he had with her.

"And so, Alex Parris," Eléna continued, "if you have all this experience, as you say, then I would have to say you were, last night, rather...mmm...inadequate? So perhaps you prefer to be inexperienced? Then I rate you 'good' with potential. You did have enthusiasm."

"All right, inexperienced. But with talent. You said so. Raw talent. You can mold it into something spectacular, Eléna." He was trying to lighten the proceedings. That was what he always did when a girl criticized him.

"Talent? What does that matter?"

The woman seemed older, suddenly, more parental in the light of day.

What the hell happened last night? He recalled the night of passion and became aroused again.

"I meant that you have potential," said Eléna. "A lot of young men have potential. Many of them waste it on useless things. I have seen it happen. They play these games and try to make victories and defeats, scorekeeping their lives. I see that in you, Alex Parris. Already you are making a tally. Here is 'one' for Eléna, yes? Who will be next? If you have this potential, where is it? Show me. Be more than a hard penis. Otherwise, stick with playing your computer games."

Alex instinctively turned away, hiding his softening crotch from her view.

"Computer games?" He suddenly regretted telling her about his future plans. It did not sound too impressive the way he described what he hoped to do as his career. Anyway, he was a long way from last night now.

"You have great imagination," she said, seemingly uninterested.

"It's not child's play," he attempted to explain. "It's a business. It's my job—or, it will be soon. As soon as I get home from this trip. The job is waiting for me. And it's a real job. I should be making at least thirty grand a year to start. It's also creative—like being a writer or artist. I use a computer to tell stories. Actually, what I write allows you, the gamer, to write your own story—within the perimeters of the game, of course."

He watched her as he spoke, and saw a glimmer of ease flash at the corners of her face. Perhaps she was tired of fighting, he wanted to believe.

"And what story will you write about us?" she asked.

"Well, these games aren't exactly love stories. They're mostly fighting."

"Then you will likely be alone in your fantasy," and she pursed her lips, off to one side, the way she did to show she was playing with him. He noticed that quirk already.

"But now I have you, Eléna," spoke Alex in a quiet, hesitant voice.

The glance she shot at him would have hurt if it were any sharper.

"I am not here to play your games!" Eléna roared. "I am not looking for anything. Nor anyone. I want to be in limbo now. Do you not understand?"

She stared at him until he looked away.

"Okay," said Alex.

"You said you want to see some old city, some rocks. You want to be someone like that. It is not for me. What I want is silks and satins, not dirty rocks and old bones. Can you not understand that?"

He buckled his belt, sat on the corner of the bed to put on his boots.

"But you had that," he said, softly. "Before."

Eléna was quiet. She quickly turned away to stare at herself in the mirror.

After their night together, he did not understand how they could begin arguing. Unless she simply enjoyed arguing with him. Anything to provoke him.

"I'm sorry, Eléna," he whispered.

"You are a silly boy! You know nothing!"

She seemed to be sobbing.

Alex stood and went to her but she turned away, pouting. He recognized the act. Suzie Meyer had done the same thing when he went to apologize to her for his frat brothers' misbehavior. She had acted as though it was his entire fault.

"You make love with me and you can say such cruel things to me?"

Alex thought she might slap his face if he stood closer.

"I apologize. It was the wrong thing to say."

She raised her eyes to him, a tear slipping out of one corner.

"You are forgiven…for this one time," she told him.

He breathed deeply, and finished lacing his boots as

Eléna watched.

"Tonight," she spoke up, "you must make even more passionate love to me. To show me your devotion. It must be very special erotic play. I will not be satisfied with last night's effort. You must give me your full potential. You must *fuck* me better than ever."

The words hung in the air like cheap perfume. She stared at his suddenly tight trousers and he wanted to turn away but did not.

The words caught in Alex's throat. "I promise."

"Then let us go."

Eléna took his hand firmly and led him out the door.

CHAPTER 5

When he tried to hold the tourist map in front of his hips, Eléna pulled his arm away. He was embarrassed but he could not keep her evening plans out of his mind as they went from site to site around Istanbul: to the Blue Mosque where the lines were too long, to the Basilica Cistern where street vendors were too persistent and disruptive, then on to the Kariye Museum which had air conditioning yet not enough ancient artifacts to please Alex, and finally to the Arkeoloji Muzesi—the national archeology museum—where his appetite for various Ilium knickknacks was whetted. Everywhere they went, Eléna always led, taking him by the hand: sometimes like his mother, frequently like his lover, too often like a prized possession she wanted to show off in public. Alex was dreaming of how Eléna's hand had felt in his hand, or how it had felt wrapped around his erection, how gentle she had been in her attention—

This time it was a large, warm hand, coarse and sweaty, that was brushing his cheek to stir him awake.

"This man…police," said the voice he recognized as the

doctor. "Police man…umm, talk to you."

Alex pulled his mind back from the days he spent touring Istanbul with Eléna, alarmed to find himself in a hospital bed once more.

"I didn't do anything," Alex exclaimed automatically. "Honest. I was just lost."

A conversation in Turkish ensued, followed by the doctor's voice: "This police man want…talk to you about…umm, you fall down. Umm, *how* you fall down."

"But I *didn't* fall down, like I've been trying to tell all of you," said Alex. "I'm not *that* clumsy. I don't even drink…much. Just a sip or two. They always made me the designated driver. Good ol' Alex. He doesn't drink. Let him drive. Everybody depended on me to be the designated driver."

There was some confused bickering between the doctor and the policeman. Alex heard a nurse intervene.

"Designated…why?" the doctor asked him finally.

"Because—because somebody has to drive everyone home!" Alex burst in frustration.

"You driving car?" the doctor asked, surprise in his voice.

"After everyone goes out drinking, somebody has to drive them all home," the patient explained, not fully realizing where he was.

Alex guessed what he heard next was the doctor's translation to the policeman. The kibitzing of the nurse and the gruff snarl of the policeman followed it.

As they talked among themselves, Alex felt faint. He felt himself slowly slipping into unconsciousness, remembering the nightmare he had, the part before he dreamed of Eléna holding his hand. Then he was stashed away beneath a haystack, miles from this coastal clinic, hiding from the police. Nevertheless, he had done nothing wrong.

He could not recall the details very clearly but he was spiraling downward as howling winds became deathly calm, and the curtain of darkness was stitched together with a million flecks of fire. There was a cave—beneath the waves, under the rocks, some place down there, and it burrowed deep into the earth. He could see it in his mind. A river of green sludge was there for him to cross, which he did, stepping gingerly along a bent pipe that protruded from one wall of the cave and stretched across to the other. Alex thought of Hades: this poor Charon, the boatman, did not pole his craft across the River Styx. No, in *his* Hades, it was an old mangled cat who purred his attention away from the hoard of rats that had been pursuing him the whole length of the death-stench Underworld.

And in a dank alcove of the cave he had collapsed, exhausted, and through the swirling lights—from stars, or suns, or moonlight, or the lanterns of villagers searching for him, he did not know which it was—he saw her: his *grandmother*, the last person he would have expected to meet in a dream. She appeared as she had been on the day she died: pale and puritanical, ever the church lady, the righteous matron who shunned social scandals like vegetarians avoided tripe. That was a revelation to him: the old woman was at least ten years older than his grandfather was. Was it an omen? Did that mean he was meant to be with Eléna? His grandmother stood, wearing the ancient Greek robes called *peplum*, and spoke solemnly to him, almost drowned by the stiff drone of Hades' captive spirits. She told him in an echoing monotone that he should get himself back to California, take his good job, make his measure of success, find a wholesome girl to bear his children, and pray every night for a clean heart and a guiltless soul.

"Grandmother," Alex had called, "I would've thought you'd say something different—I mean, something new that I hadn't heard before—what with this occasion to address me all the way from the Underworld."

He saw the shadows shift behind her like swaying curtains and the dimly lit stage became a bright, sun-drenched amphitheater, a Greek *odeon* where a man also dressed in an ancient robe was giving a speech on oral hygiene—

Whoa! Alex suddenly felt the sting of salt water splashing his face, covering his face. He thought he was drowning. Instead, he was falling—upward. Somehow, he was among olive trees, under their shade and caressed by sultry breezes curling through the boughs. Gray granite stones were propped around him as in a cemetery. Yet it was the sight of Ilium on the hill before him that beckoned him.

"What does it all mean?" Alex mumbled.

A rush of Turkish words startled him, returning Alex to the present.

"You American?" the policeman asked through the

doctor's urgent voice.

"Huh?" Alex was still foggy.

"Police man want to know, you American?" the doctor repeated with some impatience.

Alex knew they were talking about him, even though the words were Turkish. They sounded strangely like the drunken mutterings of his fraternity buddies, and the shadows shifted to become his roommate, Nick, with a swarthy face and black, curled beard, like statues of the old Greek king, Agamemnon, that he'd seen in museums. Nick had been killed driving home from spring break six weeks before graduation, a trip Alex had reluctantly declined, citing an important paper that was due. The shadows shifted and Nick was replaced by the image of the doctor—the image of how he thought the doctor appeared.

"Designated because...," Alex started to speak, trying desperately to reconnect with the conversation. He wanted to explain more but his jaw hurt. The painkiller they had given him helped dull it, but perhaps it was wearing off now. "Because I don't drink, I guess. I never really liked the stuff."

"You come from...what country?" the doctor asked.

"I flew out of San Francisco," Alex recited in a low voice, thinking back, "so I guess I must be an American. San Francisco's in America. Is that the right answer? I mean, you *like* Americans, don't you?" There was only silence. "Well, maybe then I'm Canadian."

He felt a slap to his shoulder. Was it a warning? If so, was it a warning to shut up and not give away his nationality, or a warning simply to not be playing games with the policeman? Alex waited through their conversation for some cue.

"You American, yes?" the doctor repeated.

"Do I have to answer?"

"Yes—answer," the doctor grunted, on the edge of anger.

The policeman shouted something, too close to his ear, and Alex jerked his head away, shaking it into the sharp pain and dull ache he was trying to avoid by being still. He heard the doctor's agitated voice explaining something to the policeman, perhaps about the patient's delicate condition.

"You American, yes?" the doctor repeated, softer this time.

Alex felt a hand on his shoulder which, in that moment, became reassuring. It was the nurse's hand, he guessed, reaching for it with his own hand and feeling her fingers grasp his hand.

"If I have to answer," said Alex, "then I choose…yes."

Alex's body tightened, expecting pain in response to his answer, maybe a punch to the face. Instead, nothing happened. He listened to the three-way chatter, vaguely interested in the rise and fall of their intonation, the sounds of Turkish.

"I went to London, Paris, and Rome," Alex spoke up when no one responded. "Then I went to Athens. And on to Istanbul. I don't know where I am now."

ℌ

One morning after the policeman's visit, Alex awoke and had the urge to shift his position in the bed but found that he was stuck to the sheets. When he tried to pull himself loose, the skin on his buttocks tore and he shrieked in agony. They had treated his limbs and his face and that required him to stay on his back as much as possible. It was the constant heat and his sweating that soiled the sheets and made his skin turn to mush against the rough cloth.

To make his situation worse, he realized he had also urinated during the night and his bowels were leaking from whatever poison was in his daily meals. He wanted to cry but his eyes would not produce tears. At his shriek, nurses encircled him and carefully stripped off the top sheet; their chatter must have been complaining about the stench, he guessed. He wanted to apologize but he was in too much pain to speak. They must have been able to see his pained grimace, he believed, as they cut away his dirty gown.

"I'm sorry," he muttered, thinking he was speaking louder than he was. "I'm sorry I smell so bad." He thought of the day he visited Ilium. "I'm sorry for everything."

He lay naked on the soiled sheet, pasted to it.

A doctor arrived then, speaking in a voice Alex did not recognize. He listened to the instructions, the Turkish words sounding serious. The nurses worked more carefully, he noticed, dabbing cool, wet, cotton balls with the stinging scent of alcohol against his fragile skin as they peeled the soiled sheet away. The gasps and coughing that accompanied the operation made Alex more apprehensive, but beneath his facial bandage he could hide his embarrassing display of emotion. That was the only dignity left to him.

He was laid on a fresh bed and washed off with a sponge. Rather than try to pull a new gown on him, they stretched another sheet over his torso. One nurse, whose hands were soft, remained with him. She sat on the edge of the newly made bed, wiping sweat from his forehead. She spoke to Alex in Turkish—quietly, so that, despite his lack of comprehension, her words managed to soothe him. He focused on the woman's gentle voice and slipped into sleep once again.

Someone took his hand and held it as he dreamed—perhaps Eléna, perhaps his mother, Alex did not know. Only that comforting hand and his sleepy mind seemed to remain in existence. All the rest melted away. That was all that was left of poor Alex, the computer whiz kid from CyberAmerica, Inc. He was hearing in different voices reports of his demise. The voices floated through his head. They were filled with kind words, but the general sentiment was always the same: Alex was a well-intended failure. He had tried hard but never quite succeeded. A good kid, faithful fraternity brother, loyal son, smart student, socially awkward misfit—yes. However, what an outstanding historian! That's what they would say, Alex considered, feeling lighter than he ever had before. He thought he was rising up from his bed, hovering over the sheets, perhaps disembodied, perhaps sailing to heaven—or to Olympos. His last thought before entering unconsciousness was wishing he could brush his teeth before meeting God.

CHAPTER 6

By the next morning, Alex had figured it out. There was one particular moment when his whole world changed. He counted back to when he first felt excited to be going on this trip. It was sometime between the Friday evening when he and Eléna arrived in Istanbul and the Monday when they arrived at the site of Ilium. He had never suspected what he had been missing—as though he had been dining on salad and breadsticks all his life and finally was allowed to sink his teeth into the filet mignon and drink the Merlot and savor the truffles and caviar before a rich, decadent dessert. Such foods, he pondered with a glint of guilt, were strictly forbidden by his father, the dentist, for reasons that from this distance seemed to have less to do with health than with self-control and abstinence. However, he was a long way from home now.

Until he arrived in Athens, Alex was content to drift through his travels, and it was in Istanbul that his travels shifted into high gear. He could feel the days spinning faster, the nights becoming shorter, and hotter. His senses opened and he gorged himself on the lavish sights and sounds, the lush aromas that lifted him off the ground and the nostril-piquing stenches, and all of the spicy and pungent sensuousness of the city. The dessert of Eléna, calling to him from the bed, was there for him to finish off the day. Then, like a stubborn child, he began insisting on having dessert as the main course.

It was in the middle of his twentieth roll of film when he realized what was happening.

Eléna's curvaceous figure and her flowing black hair looked fantastic through his camera lens. The simple white blouse and the beige, flowing skirt she wore framed her in virginal purity. Despite her maternal hips, she radiated sensuality and her walk was a curling finger to every man she passed. The effervescent smiles with which she ate up the camera made his photography into art, and through his eyes the camera became a sexual organ. Pose and pose again: standing, sitting, leaning, reclining, walking—she was a model who knew how exotic she appeared. Alex saw that, liked that about her.

It was the seventeenth exposure of that roll of 36 exposures, he counted from his hospital bed. The eighteenth shot would have been from the *top* deck of the Bosporus ferry. He had no idea now where his camera was, however; his pack containing the exposed film was lost. He distinctly remembered those shots because of the stares they had gotten from the other passengers. Just another vulgar American couple, they were probably thinking. Let them enjoy being bawdy for a few days then go quickly home. These Americans—so ugly, so self-absorbed, so foreign, like they own the whole world. Let's bomb some sense into them!

"Am I one of those Ugly Americans?" he had asked Eléna, lowering his voice.

"No, you are very handsome," she had responded, pressing herself into his shoulder, forcing herself into a loose embrace. "And we are a beautiful couple."

"I mean, like a bad tourist? I don't think I'm doing anything wrong."

"All tourists are bad. Do you not know that fact?" She stretched up, kissed his cheek. "Nobody wants tourists. They only want the money tourists have. I see it all the time in Athens." She gave his hand a squeeze. "It is a kind of prostitution. We are selling our homeland, the precious treasures, our most private parts for your money."

Alex released her hand. The Turkish passengers were staring at them, especially three tough-looking young men who seemed alternately entertained or decidedly puzzled by the couple's behavior. Alex stared back, without defiance, as he held Eléna's waist tighter. He tried to kiss her, but her lips darted playfully away.

"It is all a marketplace, or a shopping center," Eléna went on from the safety of his embrace. "You like what you see, you buy it. Name your price. It's all for sale."

"I can see that," said Alex. "We used to go down to Monterrey. To the beach there. In California. Great place, but the people just wanted us to leave our money at the roadside. Look but don't touch, then get the hell away. So we ended up going down to San Diego most summers. There they don't care what you do, just as long as you pay for it."

Eléna was laughing, but Alex felt anxious. He wanted to quit the tour and return with her to the hotel. He held her closer, as if assuring himself that she really was with him and would not go away.

"We have such a beautiful temple here." Eléna's laugh turned strange as she began gesturing like a tour guide. "You pay us, we show it to you. Even if you are not a believer, even if you will profane it, we will take you inside. We need the money."

Alex chuckled, decided he was jealous of her. He could never act so silly.

"In America, we don't need beautiful temples," Alex rebutted. "We have Disney World and the Grand Canyon."

"Perhaps you are ugly *here*, Alex Parris. Yet not in our bed, at least."

Eléna leaned back in his arms and glanced curiously at the other passengers, and gave a kick to the empty film box Alex had dropped. It flittered between the posts of the railing, down into the dark waters of the Bosporus. Alex gasped at her blatant littering. She reached for his face, holding it firmly in her hands and rose up on her toes to burrow her tongue into his mouth. He closed his eyes as she pulled away.

"I enjoy being ugly with you, Alex Parris!"

Alex glanced at the trio of men, and then spoke softly to her. "My dear, I think the natives are getting restless."

"Do not be worried." She looked around at other passengers. "Am I truly your dear?"

He had no answer for her. Rolling his eyes as if in thought, he beat a quick retreat to the sanctuary of history.

Before even one minute of lecture on the Byzantine economy had passed, Eléna slid her hand down to his butt, leaving it pressed between his pants and the railing of the ferry.

"Shall we continue this decadent lifestyle?" Eléna questioned him, a hint of regret in her voice. "Or should we go straight to the confessional?"

"What's there to confess?" Alex grinned. He squirmed against the railing, her hand caught between it and his pants.

She stared at him. "You fuck me with your eyes."

They indulged in another tightly groped, ugly kiss.

"Someone should take pictures of us," Eléna laughed upon parting lips.

"Do you know, you are *exquisite* through my camera lens?" said Alex. "I can't believe I get to fuck this woman. I can't believe she fucks *me*. And I never use that word."

"Which word? 'Believe'?"

Eléna's fingers tickled his backside and he restrained a giggle.

"No, the word 'fuck'."

"I love to hear you say it. It turns me on. Say it for me."

"Fuck," he spoke in a soft voice.

"Louder, Alex Parris."

"Fuck," he said, only a little stronger.

She danced away from him, posing in front of the passengers. "Alex, photograph me!"

So he took pictures of her: Eléna leaning against the support column, Eléna by the coffee vendor, Eléna gazing wistfully at the Bosporus just as she had done on the cruise ship, Eléna smiling in a strange way she never did whenever the camera was put away. Then: Eléna, standing against the ferry railing with the skyline of Istanbul rising behind her exactly as they were passing the magnificent Hagia Sophia mosque. As he was loading a new roll of film, she wrapped her leg around his, and pressed her hip against his groin.

"When we are inside Hagia Sophia," she whispered into his ear, "I want to suck you. Inside the mosque—"

"I told her I didn't think it was such a good idea," Alex explained from his fresh hospital bed. "I mean, it's such a great, historic building, and a religious monument, too. What was she thinking?"

"Tell me," said the doctor, laconically.

"I don't know," said Alex. "Every time I thought I was figuring her out, she'd change."

He wondered what the doctor, whose English was limited, thought of his story. Maybe he thought it was one of his patient's good days. Alex was not quite sure how many days he had been there. Counting good days among them was easy: two, maybe four. Apparently, God was not ready to welcome him.

"By then, I just couldn't live without her. It was more than her name—though that was what first told me that our meeting was fate. Helen or no Helen. I could live with the name *Eléna*—just as long as *she* was attached to it. So what if she didn't want to play that role in this drama? I can change it, if necessary. History is rewritten all the time, you know. It's just like plugging in some applet to patch the code. I've done it hundreds of times writing software. If there's a bug in an application, you don't start over from scratch, you just patch it and go on. Right, Doc? You don't go straight for a new heart without first trying to fix the old one. Am I right?"

A woman's voice that responded to his inquiry.

"Oh," he said, realizing the doctor had left.

The nurse took his pulse, checked his IV.

"So those guys…they followed us when we got off the ferry," Alex continued, happy to have someone, anyone to talk to. It did not matter to him if the anonymous person nearby understood any of it.

By the time he and Eléna had reached the outer walls of the famous Topkapi Palace, the young men from the ferry were nonchalantly positioning themselves between his camera and his model. Alex knew they were trying to disrupt his photography but he feared a confrontation. Therefore, he acted dumb, played the stupid tourist. He gestured at them to move over, *always* politely, and in a non-threatening manner. He was careful only to *imply* that they were in his way. He did not have much luck with that strategy.

"So I went to Plan B," he went on, contentedly. "I put away my camera."

He and Eléna made a sharp right turn and were off to tour Topkapi Palace. Alex paused at two different street corners as they went, checking whether any of the men were following. At the first street, the Turks stood in a line across the sidewalk and stared defiantly at the nasty foreign couple. That was all. Alex was relieved; he did not need to demonstrate his lack of fighting skills to Eléna. A couple of his frat brothers had been into boxing and his parents had been horrified when he came home one weekend with a black eye. That was not his sport, he realized. He had considered karate lessons, too, but his father feared damage to his son's perfect teeth. Still, Alex sensed Eléna's disappointment. She kept looking back for their stalkers.

"I met her in Athens," he told the next person to stop by his bed. The person was changing his bandages. "She was from Greece," he lied. He was no longer comfortable with the ordinariness of being an American. Eléna was born in Greece, he rationalized, so she was Greek. Nobody needed to know that she was living in the United States.

He sighed, suddenly wondering what percentage of Eléna's coolly elaborate story was true. He remembered her saying she grew up in and around Athens, and moved to America as a young adult. If she could tell tales, Alex considered, he was free to elaborate on his own life. That story of hers about a husband and two children? Was that just a fabrication to put off a crazy young fool?

Alex heard the constant "uh-huh" and "hmmm" from his otherwise silent companion so he continued.

"We were just holding hands," he said. "Okay, maybe we kissed, or we were groping each other like teenagers—but we *thought* we were out of sight. We weren't trying to shock anybody. Well, maybe *she* was. I could sense that sometimes, like maybe she was trying to provoke them. Maybe she was bored and just wanted something exciting to happen."

He caught himself. It was as though he had spied

something in the background of a photograph he had taken, a detail he had missed while the camera was up against his eye yet was now quite clear in the printed picture. It was not a photographic detail—he couldn't see yet, anyway, with the bandages over his eyes. No, it was a memory detail. Eléna had been trying to shock them. That was her entertainment.

"My dad's credit card is maxed out now," he said, adding a sigh. "I sure did buy a lot of things in Istanbul. Some of them just to please Eléna. It made her happy."

Alex realized that he was alone again. His nurse, or whoever had spent time with him, had departed. He continued anyway; someone in the ward might listen:

"In Hagia Sophia we were the perfect tourists. Then we made love back in our hotel room. Thought you'd want to know. The next day we left Istanbul together on a new tour. We headed down the coast to Çanakkale, on the road to Ilium, to see the site of the Trojan War."

&

Alex awoke suddenly, feeling the sheet wet against his thighs. As his dream washed over him and spilled away, he realized that he was being paid back for his sins. He knew he had lied to the doctor but for once he did not feel guilty. *In Hagia Sophia we were the perfect tourists*, he had told the doctor. Alex could not tell him the truth.

When the short, swarthy man in the uniform again raised the small flag for the tour group to follow, Eléna hooked her fingers under Alex's belt and held him back as the others moved on. Their clicking footsteps and the guide's monotone lecture bounced around the cavernous interior of the Byzantine church. Alex twisted away, determined to pay attention to the commentary his ticket had paid for, but Eléna took his hand and led him out of sight.

She found an alcove, barely a niche in the wall, open to anyone who happened to walk by but not part of the main tour route. She shoved Alex backwards into it. There she let her mouth ravage his face before she dropped to her knees and opened his pants. His erection rose as his pants fell to his ankles. He tried to hold them up. Eléna was there to keep him warm. Alex listened nervously to the clashing echoes of the guides' unintelligible words off in the distance. He heard a new tour group approaching.

As their voices grew closer he worried they would be discovered. It was her idea, he would explain. She pulled him into the alcove; he tried to resist but could not. The tour group was too near. Alex could not wait; he had to escape—no matter how she was making him feel. Just as he thought the tour group was arriving, there around the opposite side of the massive stone column, the huge mosque fell quickly silent and Alex let out an anxious sigh, relieved at last.

He was catching his breath when Eléna rose and planted her mouth on his. When he tried to turn away, she held his head back against the stone wall and forced her tongue into his mouth. Finally parting, Alex rushed to zip up his jeans as Eléna pressed a tissue from her purse to a conspicuous spot on the stone floor.

With his heart racing, he glanced around as she stood up, the crumpled tissue in her hand. Their eyes met for a second: his were shocked, hers playful.

She burst into laughter. He whipped his hand over her mouth and led her quickly away.

CHAPTER 7

His routine was set: sleep during the daytime and stay awake brooding through the night. Alex couldn't sleep with the others snoring or moaning in pain, anyway. He often slid into sleep nevertheless, and that left him at the mercy of both his dreams and nightmares. The steady din of the nurses' activity during the day, however, helped him relax. It also helped disrupt his self-pity sessions. He was not used to feeling pity for himself. He thought back to the last time he had been at the top of his game, spouting knowledge to an impressed audience.

"Of course there were probably good economic reasons to wipe Troy off the face of the earth," Alex was explaining to the elderly couple he shared the dinner table with on the cruise ship the first evening—before he summoned the courage to speak to that mysterious Greek woman he'd seen.

It was the same talk he had given at the *Lambda Chi* house after the Homecoming party his junior year. Three in the morning and everyone was drunk except him. As newly elected vice-president, Alex Parris had rapped his knuckles hard against the empty keg to get everyone's attention, and then proposed that, as a Greek organization, they should at least have a basic understanding of Greek civilization. With a captive audience of mostly passed-out brothers, there were no objections and Alex had proceeded to explain the causes of the Trojan War.

The elderly couple hung on his every word.

"The Trojans guarded the entrance to the rich trading lands of the Black Sea, blocking the Greeks from sailing there. So, in the greater scheme of history, it was more likely an economic-based war than one intended to revenge a royal seduction."

Alex had paused to take a few bites of his dinner, some kind of fish, seeing how the couple resembled his grandparents.

"But the seduction of Helen by Paris—made all the more easy for him thanks to the influence of the goddess Aphrodite, whom Paris chose as being the most beautiful among her, Hera, and Athena when they had a contest—are you following? It gets complicated. That was always a more interesting version to storytellers such as Homer. I mean, how else could some weak, effeminate youth win the heart of this older, married woman—a woman with children, whose famous beauty survived her aging? He needed the help of the gods! That's what is important to remember."

The three of them adjourned to the lounge, where the couple offered to buy him a drink. He shyly refused so they asked if he was old enough. Alex told them he was, but he still hesitated when they handed him a cold glass of Greek beer. To be polite he sipped it as he continued relating the story that had started it all, practically reciting his memorized A+ history paper:

"'For the Fairest,' said Eris at the wedding of Peleus and Thetis, as the uninvited guest tossed a golden apple among them and announced that the fairest of the goddesses should take it. Hera, Aphrodite, and Athena each claimed the beauty prize for herself but because a quarrel erupted between them, Zeus commanded Hermes to lead them all to Paris, the young son of King Priam of Troy. Paris was only a shepherd boy then, watching the sheep on the pastures of Mount Ida. When the three goddesses came to Paris and asked him to choose, Hera promised him a kingdom over all men; Athena promised victory in war; and Aphrodite promised him Helen—as though Helen was hers to give, hmm? He was no fool: being a young man, he decided in favor of Aphrodite and sailed to Sparta to fetch Helen. And, you know, the weird thing is...Peleus and Thetis, the couple who had the wedding that Eris interrupted? They were to become—get this!—the parents of Achilles! We all know that at the end of the war, it is Paris who kills Achilles by shooting an arrow into his heel. How's that for irony?"

Late into the night, Alex had explained everything to the couple's satisfaction, until they were making excuses to bow out. Eventually, only Alex remained in the lounge, nursing the now warm beer.

In had walked Eléna, stepping right up to the bar, not looking around, asking for a nightcap of some kind. He had watched her sitting at the bar, noticing how she stroked her index finger around the rim of the glass. He wanted to go up to her and say something but the lounge was not his territory. Instead, he had slipped out, too shy to speak to her though he very much wanted to. He made his way wearily to his stateroom. He fumbled in his pocket for the key.

Opening the door had caused him to flash back to that night of the Homecoming party when, after delivering his lecture to his drunken brothers, he had gone up to his room and found Frank Torres using his bed. Frank's companion was *the* Suzie Meyer, and it was not quite a month after she and Alex had made love in the back seat of his father's car. That was his first time. He was clumsy, and he apologized for his clumsiness. She had seemed satisfied—with his sincerity. When Alex peeked in on her and Frank, the passionate couple did not notice him, nor did they see him depart without a word spoken. He had returned to that same back seat of the car to catch some sleep. If he hadn't been so obsessed with his history studies, he would've been up to bed earlier and probably avoided or prevented that upsetting scene. They would have had to go elsewhere to betray him—

Seeing the sorry episode again, now from a hospital bed in Turkey, Alex contemplated his obsession.

Indeed, what did a young man without any cares like Paris need of a kingdom, or of victory in war? What he desired as a healthy young man was, quite naturally, a woman—but not just any woman. She had to be the fairest of mortals, the internationally famous Helen, the supermodel poster pin-up gal of her day, she with the thousand-ship launching face.

Alex, too, had no need of political gain, or victory in military struggles—he could easily manufacture those through his computer skills. An exciting career of attainable challenges, a nice but well-stocked modern apartment, a new car that was neither the most expensive nor the most fuel-efficient, and someone special to share it with: an outwardly wholesome girlfriend who was active in bed—and only his bed. That was what he wanted at this point in his life, and for the foreseeable future. Where was Eris now when he needed a golden apple and a trio of goddesses? Compared to the happy-go-lucky ancient Paris, however, Alex was broke, bankrupt, and alone. He had no goddess to watch over him or offer him the most beautiful woman on Earth, or make people go to war for him. He had the promise of a great job from a corporate recruiter when he returned, of course. Perhaps some minor goddess had helped line that up, he thought. He had to report there on Monday, August 15, at 9 a.m. sharp. No doubt his mother was already laying out his suit and tie.

His mouth tightened, teeth grinding together, as he contemplated his fate from the confines of his hospital bed.

When Paris arrived at the palace of Menelaus in Sparta to fetch Helen, he did not simply declare that Aphrodite said he could have Helen. He acted like any regular visitor and, as custom dictated, he was entertained by Menelaus, Helen's lucky husband. Menelaus was lucky in that he had won Helen in a bet with other kings such as Odysseus and his own brother, Agamemnon. After nine days of festivity, though, Menelaus left on a trip to Crete. Then Paris persuaded Helen to go off with him to Troy. Some versions of the story say Paris kidnapped Helen, took her against her will, while others say that he seduced her and made her fall in love with him. Some versions have her feeling tired of being an abused wife, or she was simply ready to start an exciting new drama, perhaps return to youthful adventure. All the stories generally agree that she already had children by then, though the couple apparently did not make the trip to Ilium with the kids in tow. Who can really say the reasons she gave up everything she had for a fling with this young prince, a shepherd boy who was merely a pawn of the gods? For Alex, nothing short of glorious romantic love, the joining of fateful soul mates, could have caused these two lovers to be together. It was Fate. It had to be. When Menelaus returned to Sparta and became aware of what they considered Helen's abduction, he persuaded his brother Agamemnon to muster an army against Troy, an army of those warriors who had been fighting each other previously, an army of all the great heroes from Achilles to Odysseus.

Alex carefully—slowly—sat up in the hospital bed, easing off the sheet and breathing deeply, anxiously. The room was stale and his bedshirt had become soaked with sweat. He could not stop thinking about his fate, no matter how hard he tried to kick the story out of his head. The more it replayed repeatedly through his restless nights, the more Alex saw that his own adventure was a strange corruption of Homer's tale of war and treachery merged with the subsequent wanderings of Odysseus.

Did Helen go freely with Paris, or was she under the magical spell of the gods? Or, was she, like Paris, merely a pawn in their heavenly game of mortal manipulation? Did she go with Paris because she craved a return to what Eléna called "flagrant youth," as Alex suspected after their first night together, or was Helen fleeing a disagreeable situation she had endured in the House of Menelaus? What was Eléna running from? How could Alex have been in the proverbial right place at the right time? Was Eléna his for the asking, some reward given by long-hidden gods? What had he done to deserve her? He stared into the night. Did he deserve her? Did he deserve anything? There would be no conclusion to the inquiry, Alex knew, because there were no clues to her heart. That Menelaus wanted Helen back, even after she had given herself to the foreign boy, was widely reported. Even those citizens who had sent their sons and husbands to fight and die for ten years at Troy to win her return welcomed her back as the victim of a vile act and pitied her for the remainder of her life.

"The lives of mortals meant nothing to the gods," Alex mumbled in the dark, his heart beating quickly, his body covered in sweat. "After all, they were all safe in their fucking pantheon."

Hearing his voice both startled him and reassured him that he was actually awake and not lost in a dream. That, however, left him with the conclusion that he had lost his mind. The gods had the power to drive men crazy, he had read. However, gods like those did not exist, had never really existed. Just stories designed to illustrate customs and explain the forces of nature. His mother had insisted on his church attendance to learn about one kind of god and his parents mistook his interest in Middle Eastern history to be a good sign of his theological correctness. Someday soon, he would prove them wrong, he vowed.

Alex tried to stretch his body, his arms and legs, and for a few moments he believed he was safely tucked into his childhood bed at home.

"I understand now," he spoke to himself. He always thought he knew how the pieces of the puzzle fit together. Now, however, perhaps aided by the wonderful drugs and his dire circumstances, it was all so clear to him—at long last. The fate of Western civilization hinged on that ten-year war. The outcome shifted the center of civilization from the Middle East to what would be called Europe. The rest is history, as they say. Only Alex seemed to understand that. From that ancient war, the millennia-long direction of the modern era was decided, for better or worse. Sometimes war is good. Sometimes the struggles and conflicts of humanity turn out to be for the greater good, even if some people suffer and die. It was a cleansing fire, a baptism of fire, a rite of passage from youth to adulthood on the lifespan of history. It was not a pleasant epiphany for Alex, but in the resolution of the conflict he was able to relax and sleep.

Soon he awoke, realizing that night existed only beneath the bandages that covered his eyes and that outside of them the world was awake and bustling. All he could do, though, was listen. He sank into his pillow and willed away the past few days of dreamy existence, trying to understand what had happened. He remembered the big, white car—and the cold bottle of beer. He could now remember his head being struck hard on the side. That sent him spinning off into a dizzying dream world. And the flash of light just before he lost his sight. The rest was dust and noise.

CHAPTER 8

Alex floated above the clouds, gazing down through them, examining the maps in his dreams. There near the Hellespont, spread across a plain divided by the rivers Xamander and Simois, lay Ilium, the capital city of the kingdom of Troy which commanded the upper Aegean and ruled the passage to the Black Sea. He was muttering something about the descendants of Minoa founding Troy, fleeing the island of Crete when Thera's volcano exploded in 1626 B.C. Therefore, they were cousins of the Achaeans they would fight four hundred years later. He asked questions and answered them, insisting that the inhabitants of Troy were originally settlers from Assyria. Troy's king, Priam, had a half-brother, Tithonus, who ruled the province of Assyria on behalf of the conquering Persians. Tithonus sent his son, Memnon, with a thousand warriors from Ethiopia to fight on the side of Troy.

"What's he talking about?" a man's tenor voice spoke outside of Alex's bandages.

The doctor spoke and Alex paused, realizing he had been semi-conscious and mumbling. He listened to the clinic's usual noises, focused on a dry hacking cough a few beds down. The man had been that way all night, though Alex had little knowledge about the changing of the hours. He sensed people beside his bed. After his experience with the policeman's interrogation, he was apprehensive, afraid to move or let on that he was awake now.

"Is English," the doctor's plain baritone spoke. "He talks …in the sleep."

Alex felt a warm breath near his ear.

"Can you hear me?" asked the voice of America with a distinctly Southern accent.

"No," the patient responded automatically. He still had to act semi-conscious, he decided. That was the best way to get through these interrogation sessions.

"Can you tell me your name?"

"What?" Alex asked, acting as though he was slowly coming out of his dream. Perhaps he really was just coming out of it. The maps in his head still swirled vividly, a few clouds blocking his view. He was lower now, ready to land.

"Do you understand English?"

Alex listened carefully to the accent in the voice. There was something disturbing about it, so he replayed it in his mind.

"Are you an American citizen?" the voice asked with a hint of eagerness. Alex could identify the voices of each of the four nurses in the ward, his doctor, the night medic, and the two orderlies. This man was not one of them.

"Who are you?" Alex dared to ask.

"I'm Lieutenant Capelli, U.S. Navy," his visitor spoke,

enunciating each word for the patient. "Call me Vince." Alex sensed the man's smile. "I've come to see that you get some proper medical treatment. That is, if you're an American."

"If I'm American…?"

"Yes. Because, like I said, I'm from the U.S. Navy." Alex was silent and the officer must have thought he couldn't understand his words. "We can't treat you if you're some other nationality. I mean, if you're British, they'd send you to a British facility."

"Okay," Alex muttered, not sure if he understood the question.

"I need to ascertain whether or not you're American," the lieutenant continued. "If you're not, we'll need to notify the appropriate authority, that is, a consulate or diplomatic mission."

The Turkish doctor spoke to the visitor, and Alex heard the lieutenant speaking Turkish back to the doctor, but with a Texas drawl. It sounded to him as though they were discussing what to do with him, deciding his fate. Like a pair of gods.

"The doctor here tells me you had no papers on you when you were found," Lt. Capelli spoke to him. "Can you tell me what happened to you?"

"Happened?" That was all he had thought about since arriving at the clinic, but now his mind was blank. He just appeared one day in this hospital bed. Everything before Ilium was an abstract painting. After Ilium was—

"Do you know how you got here?"

Alex tried to sit up, felt his head splitting, and fell back.

The doctor called a nurse who applied a wet towel to his forehead. A stream of water ran down his forehead, under his bandages. It tickled at first, then felt good.

"Last thing I remember was kissing Eléna.... No—that was earlier. That was Istanbul. Then we went to Ilium." That episode was fuzzy. Perhaps it was best that it remained fuzzy. "I guess I don't know."

"That's okay. What *do* you remember?"

"Not a whole lot."

"Do you know what year it is?"

"I think it's...ninety-three." His voice reflected doubt. "Right?"

"Yes. Very good."

"Thanks." Alex breathed a sigh of relief.

"So...how did you lose your passport?" the lieutenant asked.

"The Cyclops took it." Alex was not being funny. That was what they called the big, burly man with the eye patch. The constable, he recalled with a flash of joy. Well, not joy—relief that he had not forgotten everything. He was getting his mind back.

"The what...?"

By the sudden silence, Alex imagined the lieutenant was exchanging baffled looks with the doctor.

"The policeman. He had an eye patch," said Alex, "so that's what we called him. Before we...."

"Before...what?"

"Before Ilium—" and he stopped. "No—after Ilium. Everything bad happened after Ilium." Some part of his brain was functioning now, as if it had just been switched on. The trailers were ending and the warning to be quiet was showing; the mood was set for the feature film. It began with the catchy studio logo animation—

"What's Ilium?" the lieutenant questioned.

He heard the doctor quickly jump in to explain.

"You mean Troy, is that right? The ruins...."

"I don't know what happened to me," Alex muttered again, summoning his strength. The picture was fading, the camera off-kilter so the film was a split screen now. Desperate, Alex tried again to rise up but the pain in his head flattened him. "I don't know where I am. Or why I'm here," he sputtered, breathing hard. "I shouldn't have come here."

Alex still felt a dull ache in the pit of his stomach that he equated with the desire to speak more, to tell his story to the voices around him, regardless of their reaction. He was not to blame, and they needed to understand that. He was the victim.

"I thought I did everything right," Alex blurted out, interrupting the conversation between Lt. Capelli and the Turkish doctor.

"Everything? Right? What do you mean?" asked the lieutenant.

"I had my dad's credit card. I even told her I would pay for anything, whatever she wanted. That was dumb, I know, but—"

"Pay?"

"For what?"

"That's what I'm asking you. Pay for what?" said the lieutenant. "A woman you paid. Who was she? Are you talking about a prostitute? Were you robbed?"

Eléna was no prostitute. That was his first reaction, and Alex's jaw set sternly against speaking more that would involve her. He had to clear her name.

"She's not a prostitute," said Alex after a moment. He quickly assessed their brief relationship. They were lovers. There was no money involved. There was only love. And sex. Then the hot, dusty wind. "I don't know what happened to me."

However, he did know. There never was a more coherent moment for him since he was picked up from the road and brought to this clinic. There was a big, white car and a bottle of cold beer, he remembered. He normally didn't like beer but since it was cold, he drank it. Suddenly he was face-down on the dirt road. He tried to get up and walk but he found he could not take two steps. He dragged himself along the road, until he heard the bus coming and rolled out of the way.

"You don't know, or you won't say?" the lieutenant pressed.

Alex imagined a line of questioning stretching back over the past several days. It would uncover all of his indiscretions, all of his vanity. That was certainly not what he wanted. The trail might lead back to Eléna. Shouldn't he protect her? She was not involved. Besides, he was a good kid; everybody always said so.

"I won't say I don't know…."

Alex sensed the lieutenant's exasperation. For a moment, he wanted to take back his words, spoken out of a head swimming in a fantasy ocean, trying to buck the currents like the ferry when it was crossing the Dardanelles at Çanakkale. It was exhausting for both of them.

"You may not know it," said Lt. Capelli, "but you need a lot more medical attention than they can provide here. That's why they called us. They said you were found in a ditch on up the coast. Brought in on a commuter bus. Do you remember any of that?" The silence seemed to go on too long. "So say something. You want to get home, don't you?"

The lieutenant turned back to speak Turkish to the doctor, leaving Alex to wait in the darkness behind his bandages.

Alex felt dizzy. The injection they gave him before the lieutenant arrived had taken over his mind. He had to speak or the lieutenant would think he was too incoherent to bother with. Then he might never get out of this hospital. He might never find Eléna.

"You follow sports?" the lieutenant suddenly asked Alex.

"Real or fantasy?"

"I suppose real. How about football?"

The lieutenant eventually was able to establish Alex's citizenship to his satisfaction by discussing football.

"Can you tell me the losing quarterback in the past three Super Bowls?"

"I know that," said Alex. "I lost bets on all of them—against the guys in my frat house. Fifty bucks each time. I never learned. I won't bet on football anymore—"

"So what's your answer?" Capelli insisted.

"Last January, that sure was a blow-out. The sorry-ass losing quarterback was Jim Kelly, of the incompetent Buffalo Bills," said Alex, slowly gaining strength now that his mind had been poked. "I finally decide to bet on the Bills and they lose. Third time in a row. And against the Cowboys, too! Fifty-two to, I dunno, minus ten? Before that, it was the same Jim Kelly versus the Redskins, and before that, Jim Kelly again. Lost to the Giants. Before that was John Elway, Denver Broncos, who dropped a big one against the Forty-Niners...."

He continued in a steady mumble for several minutes, running down the list of losers like a speech he had memorized for some class in high school.

"All right, Alex, that's enough."

"...and Super Bowl One was Len Dawson, Kansas City Chiefs. The last of the losers. Not counting me."

"All right, I believe you, Alex. You're American. No foreigner would be so obsessed with football."

"Don't ask me about basketball or hockey. I don't know anything about them."

"I won't. Don't worry."

That arcane athletic knowledge, like a breath of wisdom from the Muses, bought Alex an air-conditioned ambulance ride away from the doctor he thought of as old King Alcinous and his lovely nurse, the king's daughter, Nausicaä, and the town clinic in Edremit. It was a step in the right direction, the start of the voyage home.

"We're going to move you to the nearest American hospital, which is the naval base at Izmir," Lt. Capelli told him before they carried him outside on a stretcher. "Then we'll get you patched up and figure a way to get you home, okay?"

"Izmir?" Alex asked, growing feverish. "That's the wrong direction."

"What're you talking about?" Lt. Capelli questioned, and the Turkish doctor apparently explained to him about the patient's delirium.

"I gotta go back to Ilium!" Alex shouted, sitting up, almost capsizing the stretcher.

He was thrust into the open door at the back of the van and two male nurses hooked him up to monitors.

"Goodbye," said the voice of his Turkish doctor, and Alex sensed he was relieved to see him go.

Alex felt a soft squeeze of his hand. It could only have been the nurse, he thought, but as the drugs worked their magic he believed it must have been, could only have been Eléna's hand, wishing him a safe journey home.

"What's home got to do with anything?" he burst out, his speech slurring. "I gotta go back to Ilium. To Eléna. To my…girlfriend."

"What's he talking about?" the lieutenant asked the doctor, who replied with a shrug of his shoulders Alex's attuned ears could hear.

"I gotta find Eléna!" Alex cried out blindly.

The nurses strapped him down.

"Have good luck," the doctor told the lieutenant, or perhaps Alex, as the doors to the ambulance were closed.

As they drove off, Alex wanted to wave farewell but he was too weak and slept the entire two-hour drive south to Izmir, dreaming all the way.

CHAPTER 9

Arriving in the third of three tour buses driving down from Çanakkale that morning, Alex and Eléna had stepped off the dust-blanketed vehicle and stood silently at the entrance to the past.

Wearing a blue plaid shirt and khaki trousers with his usual hiking boots, Alex had taken her hand and given it a gentle squeeze, a reminder of the night they spent in the Çanakkale hotel bathed in their melded perspiration, twisting in the moist sheets. Like Paris bedding Helen for the first time, Alex imagined. Today he felt they were finally lovers. Eléna, wearing a white, sleeveless top and tight blue jeans with embroidery on the back pockets, gave his hand a return squeeze. He felt the bond growing stronger between them. Confidence was blossoming in him, too, and a special kind of joy that he recognized was no longer an adolescent's simple happiness. That pleased him.

Today was to be the pinnacle of his entire trip and having his lover share it with him would heighten the experience. They would forever have this special day in their mutual memories. For a few precious hours, he would focus his attention on gathering into his mind and his soul all that he could take from this historic, even sacred, place. He would show Eléna a new world made of remnants of the old. In that way, she would be able to see his passion for ancient history and especially for the event known as the Trojan War. He still had plenty of desire for her, but today his desire was for a war. He tried to explain all of that on the bus, perhaps as a kind of warning, but his lover was content to sit beside him, arm in arm, and occasionally nuzzle against him.

Alex stared at the entrance gate. It was show time.

"The city was called Ilium," he said, stepping away from the tour bus, Eléna following, pulled by his hand. "People call it Troy today, but Troy—or what was actually the entire Troad region here in northwest Asia Minor—was the name of the kingdom that spread over the whole area here, as well as some of the islands offshore. That's the reason Homer's famous poem is called the *Iliad*, or 'song of Ilium' rather than a song of Troy."

He knew Eléna could see how awe-struck he was. He was like a child in a candy store. Her lover could teach this class without notes, straight out of his head. That had to be impressive. He was no longer the student but the teacher.

"The gods directed the mortal forces in the wars of Sumer and Palestine and Egypt before Ilium. It was like a heavenly chess match," said Alex as they strolled down the avenue leading to the stone gate entrance, "and they did so here, lording over the Aegean combatants. With good reason, too. Zeus was considered the founder of Ilium.

King Priam counted his lineage down from Zeus. Zeus was also, quite ironically, the father of Helen, by the rape of her mother, Leda. He passed Helen off as the daughter of the King of Sparta. Neat trick, huh? Adoption and all. Every one of the gods took sides in this war, each with his or her favorite warrior-champion, making it truly a family feud."

"Look at it now," said Eléna, gesturing with her bare arm across the stone bulwarks. Between the stones grew tufts of grass and weeds, some wildflowers, and brown, dry straw lay everywhere. The sun beat down on them, hot even at the mid-morning hour.

"Of course, it's just the ruins of the city now," he said, almost apologetically, "but it used to all be covered with dirt and grass. It was nothing but a hill. Nobody could see it then. Nobody even knew it was here. Then that German archeologist—Heinrich Schliemann was his name—calculated it must be around here somewhere. See, he started at Mycenae, on the Peloponnesus peninsula, which was where Agamemnon's palace was, and he got clues there. So he started to dig here in Turkey. The excavations he did were pretty rough and he actually destroyed a lot of the site before a real archeologist, a man named Dörpfeld, took it over. In fact, I read just last year that they did a complete restoration of the site, uncovering more of the city—and also undoing some of Schliemann's mistakes. They've begun a new excavation, too—a proper excavation. And here we are, right on time!"

Alex scanned the site before him: a rough, dirty hillside with beige rocks and dried vegetation here and there, along with some paper trash and a soda can blown across the path in front of them. He sighed, unexpectedly distraught. The line of other tourists passed them as he paused to take in all of it.

"Well," said Alex, "I guess we'll need to use our imagination."

Sure, the stones stood tall once again—massive blocks of granite excavated and cleared of centuries of the dirt and debris that had covered them. He saw how they could have easily shone brightly against the sunlight with their pale surfaces. The golden towers of Ilium had fallen long ago, and yet he could imagine them as clearly as if they still stood. His gaze turned skyward, seeing them rise in the morning light. Now tufts of grass grew out of the gaps and cracks among the stones lining the avenue. The paths behind and around the ancient walls had been dug out, down to the old street level and were recently covered with gravel to make it easier for tourists' shoes to remain clean as they walked through the site. A parade of wooden guideposts littered the holy past with reminders of the present.

Alex gasped, called it vandalism.

"I thought it would be…more…unkempt," he spoke, shielding his eyes as he gazed to his left, then his right. "I know they're excavating, but…this isn't what I expected."

He stopped, his eyes struck by an unholy sight. Straight ahead, rising above the souvenir kiosks, was a tall, brown wooden horse. He expelled a disgusted guffaw and shook his head.

"No, not again! The way it's going, the Disney people will be here in another year or two! Just like the big Trojan

Horse they have standing on the waterfront at Çanakkale; with a staircase leading up into its groin, and children shouting from the windows in the horse's chest, and all the stupid flowers growing around it, like it was some peace memorial instead of a war machine. This one looks even newer. And stupider. It couldn't have been built more than a couple years ago. Definitely not ancient, though they like to pretend. It's shameful. History is not about pretending. I can see it now: Turkish-Disneyland. Or the Six Flags people will transform it all! Yeah, Six Flags…*pfft!* More like twenty flags over this part of the world. Yeah, come dress up like Helen and Paris. Fight simulated battles like Achilles and Hector. Be a virtual general like Agamemnon. Be stupid and vain and heroic and dead! Hah! Be a virtual god! Virtual, yes. That's it! And I'm…I'm one of those sick bastards who's in the market to do it. Maybe I shouldn't exploit this in some computer game. It's just too—"

Eléna patted his shoulder. "The horse was in a park. A statue for them to remember the real one."

"But it's just wrong, the way they had it set up."

"Let them have their memories."

He nodded, reluctantly accepting the idea, glancing around.

"Should I drop my great ideas?" said Alex. "Or should I let stupid greedy salesmen turn them into some perversion?"

"You dream of money, yes?" Eléna asked, but Alex ignored her, caught up in his rage at how poorly the sacred site had been maintained.

They walked on, slowly, at his pace, as though they

were measuring every step. Alex was afraid if they went too quickly he might miss something important—some meaningful crack on a flagstone, a significant black burn mark on a stone wall, an important splinter perhaps from a broken spear, a useful bronze shard or a strip of leather that would lead to a moment lost in time being instantly resurrected before his modern eyes.

"Trojan Horse!" Alex exclaimed, furiously. "I know kids now who hate it—because it means nothing to them now but a computer problem, what we call a virus. I know this guy back in college who was working on software to detect them and fix them. He's gonna make a ton of money off that. But other guys I know—well, they don't even know how that kind of virus got the name. They think it's from USC." He looked at Eléna, who was studying his face as he got angry, then frustrated, then resigned to his fate, to the fate of computer technology. "That's a university in California. Their mascot is the Trojans."

"Yes, I understand it now," she said, fake delight in her voice. She playfully slapped his shoulder. "How did you know I don't understand about computer?"

"I'm sorry. I shouldn't have presumed."

"I really don't know about computer, Alex."

"Then I was right to explain it, huh?"

"Teach me, Alex."

"You know about the Trojan Horse, don't you?"

"Yes, that I know."

"About how the Greek soldiers hid inside and—"

"I want you inside, Alex," she whispered, "inside me."

"Not here—not now, Eléna." He tried to console her,

kissing her cheek. "Let's save that for tonight. Okay?"

She pouted and he remembered how he had pouted when they were in Çanakkale and people were referring to it as Troy—when it clearly was not the same place as where he now stood. The horse before him now was a sleeker, browner twin of the huge wooden horse that stood in front of the government buildings and souvenir shops. He saw the wooden planks, carefully carved by the latest machinery and painted dark brown but faded with the weather. They had been bolted together like the crossbeams of some kind of backyard playset. To add to the playset impression, children were already climbing around inside of it when he and Eléna arrived. Some of the children hung their arms and heads out the portholes, waving at and calling to their parents to take pictures. There were no portholes in the real wooden horse! Only a small trap door—in the rear, under the tail.

"And why a horse? Did anyone of those people abusing the symbolism know why?" Alex stopped and asked Eléna.

"Why, Alex? Tell me why!" She laughed. "Please tell me everything about the horses of Troy."

He grinned, his teeth catching the sunlight.

"All right, since you insist, I'll tell you. You see, the horse was the symbol of Troy, like their mascot. If they had a football team, they would probably have been called the Warhorses, or something like that. They were famous for breeding horses. The Greeks had little need of horses in their rocky, hilly landscape. Troy had room for horses to run free on the plains around the city and in the valleys, and they had a need for horses, for a chariot cavalry. In fact, Hector, the Trojan's hero, was called 'Tamer of Horses'. That was his nickname. Today he'd probably be called 'Stallion' or something. So no other image would have been accepted by the Trojans as a *gift* left by their Greek enemies, certainly not a gift worth taking inside of their city. In fact, it was so large they had to tear down the front gate to get it inside. They thought the Greek army had left, anyway, so it was safe to do that. All of that effort despite the warnings of their prophetess, Cassandra, which they all ignored. Of course, they thought she was crazy."

Eléna stretched up and kissed him and Alex felt all the eyes of the other tourists fixed on them. He wrapped his arm around her shoulders and held the kiss a moment longer. Her hand patted his crotch as they parted lips, but he only gave a smirk that suggested something fabulous would occur in their hotel room when they returned in the evening.

"The siege was ten years long," Alex explained. He remembered the previous night and how long he had pushed against her. He walked along the path with his lover. "Most people don't know it took nearly ten years after Helen's abduction before the Greeks finally arrived and started to fight. First, they sent envoys demanding the return of Helen. The so-called diplomatic solution—even though she was no longer, umm, pure. After being turned away empty-handed, the Greeks then decided to go to war. They had to gather their forces—which meant they had to send word to every kingdom, to summon every warrior, which took a helluva long time without any e-mail or fax.

And they had to build ships and make weapons and armor. They had to plan for everything, gather food supplies, and so on. Then they packed up their forces and their supplies and set sail for Troy. Then there were storms that forced them to turn back. Storms! Just when they're ready to start the big game."

"Alex, do you always speak like an old book?"

He heard the question, took it as a compliment. He was already in mid-thought so he pushed his reply back into his short-term memory for later dispensation.

"Eight years later—after countless war councils and resupplying the armies, and building more ships to make up for the ones damaged in the storms, they once again set sail—launching a thousand ships, as Homer said. And soon they arrived again on the shores of Ilium. Right over there!"

He swung his arm toward the far off coast, about five miles away. Eléna's eyes followed his hand. A thin, blue line stretched across the horizon.

"Of course, there was a large bay there, back in those days," he continued. "The river's silt has filled it up over the past three thousand years."

"Really?" Eléna asked, trying to be interested.

"Yes."

Alex noticed how she was trying to show interest. He appreciated her efforts to make him happy. He would make it up to her later, back in the hotel room.

"So, to prevent the Greek ships from landing and the warriors from disembarking, the Trojans lined up along the shore, ready to fight. The Greeks couldn't land at first so they went on around the coast and attacked other villages during the next few months, and came back later. They succeeded in putting troops ashore and the first battle began immediately. Hector, the eldest son of King Priam, struck down the Greek warrior Protesilaus and thereby set in motion the prophesy, which said that the side that lost a soldier first would ultimately triumph. It happened to come true."

"The gods never lie," Eléna whispered in his ear.

"Well, the gods have the ability to make sure that whatever the heck they prophesize will come true. That's a perk of being a god, I guess."

Eléna, nodding routinely, pulled her hand from Alex's hand and laid her arm across his lower back, leaning into his shoulder as they walked the narrow avenues of Ilium. It was almost as though she was trying to nudge him away from his obsession, he decided, or else she was trying to remind him she was still present in his world. He recognized that and loved her more. He intended to be so passionate in the evening, back in their hotel room, to reward her patience—as long as he was not tired from hiking all day. Strolling the streets here was as similar as a stroll down the Champs-Elysées, or down Fifth Avenue in New York: a simple, pleasant walk on a hot summer's afternoon with interesting shops along the way. Except here there was only rock and stone, grass and dirt, and archeological signs in Turkish and English hammered into the ground here and there—and the noisy tourist crowds milling about, unable to visualize the glory and horror which surrounded the barely one square-mile plot of land.

"It was a ten-year siege," Alex reminded her, knowing she was interested in all that he knew, "but they didn't fight every day. No, when they did fight, it might be for several days at a time, but in between the fighting and their attempts to break the siege, there was a lot of sitting around. They had to repair their weapons and armor, and tend to wounds. They called a lot of truces. On holidays, like for religious celebrations, they even got together, both sides, acting as best friends, and went to the temple to worship side by side. They would return to fighting the next day. And all the Greeks wanted was for their leader's wife to be returned. Also, some monetary compensation, of course. Had to pay for the trip, you know. Yet the people of Ilium refused. They wanted to possess the world's most beautiful woman in *their* city. I guess it would be like being known as the Miss Universe capital. And of course Paris, the kid, had to have his beautiful woman."

He caught Eléna in one arm, hinting at the connection, the parallels between old and new, and she raised her chin expecting a kiss from him. Instead, his lips kissed the air with words:

"Historians still debate whether she was kidnapped or she went willingly with him. A war started, either way." He took a breath, sensing her desire for more. "So, since the Greeks—actually, the Achaeans would be the correct name, and there were groups from many other lands of modern Greece—since they couldn't break into the walled city here, they spent time conquering all of the neighboring towns, on the mainland as well as on the island of Lesbos, off-shore over there. Those lands were all within the borders of the kingdom of Troy."

Eléna, the woman who had captivated him, who had accompanied him to this wayside clump of ruins, far off her itinerary, wrapped her arm tighter around his waist. Alex soon noticed her fingers slowly strumming his side like a guitar. He was completely happy, softening his anger at the unexpectedly grim appearance of the historical site. Eléna was fascinated by his knowledge of the events and the many players in this ancient drama, he knew. That had always been his strength: his smarts. Anything more would follow quite naturally with his clean smile and his slim, fit body. However, he never got the girl in the end, the thought occurred to him as he caught Eléna's glance.

"It's amazing to be here, isn't it?" He took a deep breath, his chest filling out. He felt ready to grab a lance and race into battle. "Here I am—at Ilium. Here *we* are."

"We are here, yes," she sighed. "Can we go someplace else?"

"We just arrived."

"I'm tired already, Alex." She pursed her red lips, but he was too busy examining the stone walls to notice. "You wore me out last night."

"What's that?" he asked, returning his attention to her.

"With all your humping and the pumping and your pushing and grinding, you made me very sore!"

"Oh, come on," he said, amused. "It wasn't that bad."

"No, it was good. Very, very good."

"We can repeat it tonight, then." He pointed ahead. "For now we need to see everything we can here."

"I see it all. I looked for ten minutes: broken stones—

dirt—grass—tourists."

"I need to see more, Eléna."

"I'm tired, Alex. We should sit and have lunch soon." Each of them was given a lunch box as part of the tour price. The boxes were back at the bus, so they would not miss it.

"All right. We'll have our lunch. In a few more minutes, okay? Then we can finish the tour. Then we can return to the hotel."

Alex walked on and Eléna exhaled her frustration and hurried to join him, taking his arm in hers.

They followed the designated path, trailing the other tourists: first stop the massive tower in the impressive stone wall of Troy VI, then around to the eastern gate, past the remains of nobles' houses constructed during Troy VI and the crumbling houses of Troy VII, the most recently inhabited level that had been excavated. As they strolled, Alex explained how Schliemann had dug straight down to the lowest level he could find, which was actually the second city of Troy. He left a big trench in his wake. The marks of fire on the walls of Troy II made Schliemann think it must have been the city that was sacked by the Greeks. In all, archeologists had discovered nine levels; the top level was a Roman city, which lasted for a few hundred years. Eventually, the hilltop was abandoned completely.

Soon they came to the Dardanian gate, which was guarded by a huge square tower in ancient times.

"According to Homer," said Alex, "from that tower, the royalty of Ilium could survey the battles on the great plain. They also would have witnessed the slaughter of their hero, Hector, by Achilles in single combat, followed by the desecration of Hector's body. You see, Achilles tied Hector's body by the ankles to the back of a chariot and dragged him around the city—"

"Shhhh," said Eléna, pushing her finger against his mouth. "You don't need to speak of war every minute."

He blinked. "Not every minute. So the armies took turns in victory on the battlefield. It was mostly crowds of fighters going at it hand-to-hand, face-to-face, what they called *aristeia*—though the Achaeans often fought in disciplined lines of interlocking shields. The soldiers—just average citizens drafted into service—they would exchange spear-thrusts with their opponents whenever the lines met. Do you know what a mess a metal spear point can make in flesh, even with them wearing armor? Here, Eléna, let me read you this."

He reached into his backpack.

"I know the story. I am Greek, yes?"

He flipped quickly through his dog-eared volume of *The Iliad*.

"Here it is: When Achilles lunges at Demoleon, one of the Trojans, Achilles, quote, *stabbed his temple and cleft his helmet's cheekpiece. None of the bronze plate could hold it—boring through the metal and skull the bronze spearpoint pounded, Demoleon's brains splattered all inside his casque*, unquote. That's tough. Can you picture it? You know, Homer called combat 'hard labor'—something to take seriously and sweat over. You wanted to be very conscientious of maintaining a high standard in your job skills. Makes sense, don't you think? I mean, a soldier who wants to merely 'get by' in his 'work'—the slacker—he'd quickly find himself slain in a most cruel and agonizing fashion, and he'd be roaring, bellowing in fatal pain! And nothing could be done. No helicopters to evac you to a M.A.S.H. unit nearby, no life-saving medical procedures. You're a six-week sea voyage from home and your family will learn of your fate only when the armies return years later. Meanwhile, your body is pounded into the dirt by the battle itself, by men's sandals, by horse hooves, by chariot wheels. And there's no formal burial for the line soldiers, only the joining of their torn flesh with the earth. Dust to dust, once again. And for what?"

Eléna tore away from him. He thought she might be crying, the way she held her hands to her face. The description had upset her, he supposed.

"It's history," he called to her. "I'm sorry. It's not always pretty."

She seemed angry—or disgusted. He could handle the gore, but he failed to consider her delicate tastes. Perhaps hearing about men killing men, especially in such gruesome ways, was not a good way to spend the afternoon. Ilium was not a date place. It was an outdoor museum, a place meant for contemplation, not flirtation. That was fine, he thought. No doubt she had her own interests which he would not want to share. He was good at compromise, so he knew they could make it work. Back home, they would have their nights out, he with the guys, she with her gal pals. The rest of the time, they would be together, sweating and groaning and wearing out the bed.

He grinned, showing his perfect teeth, and no longer felt

the heat of the sun.

CHAPTER 10

"What's his name again?"

"Alex. Parris. A civilian."

"A civilian? What's he doing here?"

"He was found up the coast, in a ditch or someplace."

"Got in some trouble, huh?"

"Looks like it."

"Alex, can you understand me?"

It was a fluent English voice that called him, a deeper and richer one this time. The voice was soothing but the taint of cigar smoke tickled his nose. His parents had forbidden any smoking in the house and when he was caught trying a cigarette he was grounded for a month. He was stuck in his room.

"What happened to you?" asked the man.

The last thing Alex could recall was riding in a car with some men who were going to help him. That is what they said. They were going to take him to Eléna. Or were they? It all went blank. How long had he been in this darkness?

He opened his eyes, saw the blackness beneath the bandages, and listened.

"Alex, I'd like to take a look at your eyes. Is that all right?"

He remained motionless and silent.

"I know you can hear me. Do you understand? It's all right, Alex. I'm the eye doctor here."

"Doctor...?" Alex mumbled. He was unsure if he had actually spoken or merely thought the word.

"Yes, I am."

There was a pause. Alex could sense hands hovering over his face.

"I'll have to remove the bandages, so it'll be bright. Here, let me shield your eyes."

"Who—?"

"Who am I? I'm Commander Johnson, a Navy doctor. Naval Reserve, actually."

"Oh...."

"Do you know where you are?"

"Ilium?"

"No, Izmir."

"I gotta go back...."

"You can go home soon enough, young man. Anyway, I need to check your eyes now. Are you ready?"

"Don't think so," Alex moaned, realizing there was a dull ache growing in the center of his head.

"Do you know what happened to you, how you got so beat up?"

"I—think I—was—"

"Yes...?"

"—beat up."

"Ah...yes. Well, they sure did a number on you."

"What—number?"

He waited for an answer, any answer, and grew more worried when it didn't come quickly.

"Alex, I'm not going to sugar-coat it," said the doctor finally. "Whoever did this to you did a good job of it. You want to hear about it now? Or can it wait? I just came to check your *eyes*. Other doctors will deal with the rest of your injuries."

Alex raised his hand, felt it embraced by a metal splint. He was trying to point a finger—he did not know which one—to signal something.

"Are you sure you want to know?"

"Tell me," Alex finally blurted out, as though it took all the strength he could gather to get those two words out. His arm dropped to the bed.

"All right, young man," said Dr. Johnson. "First, let's see your chart. Looks like you took a good blow to the head, in front of your ear: it's cracked. Jaw, too." Alex cringed, fearing the doctor would tap on it like the Turkish doctor had done. Nothing happened—only the continuing list of his injuries: "Says they wired it back in wherever you came from. In addition, you have a broken right arm, wrist and elbow. You probably guessed that from the cast. There's some nerve damage around the elbow, too. Seems it was twisted the wrong way. Are you right-handed?"

Alex tried to nod, felt the pain in his head, and returned to raising a finger for 'yes'. He heard the doctor sigh, followed by the sound of a door opening and swinging shut with a rough, grinding noise. He thought of the door of the bus when he was rescued from the dirt road, from the dust-lined ditch—

"We can work on that later, son. Plenty of therapy available. Moving right along...here's a broken ankle, right side—more of a big crack, I guess. Looks like your right kneecap's busted, too. That's what your chart says. The good news is all of those problems can be fixed."

"There's more," a woman's voice spoke.

Alex heard the doctor raise the top sheet of the report at the nurse's instruction.

"Oh, there's a second page." More rustling of paper. "And page three."

"Quite a litany," another man's voice cut in.

"Three ribs cracked—not broken, I should point out," said Dr. Johnson. "And the usual bruises, scrapes. Some cuts, a couple serious ones—by a knife, looks like. In fact, you had a rather deep puncture wound in your abdomen. Apparently, it perforated the colon above your hip, but Doctor Lindsay here stitched that right up."

"How're you doing, Alex?" asked the man named Lindsay.

"As I said, young man, all of that can be fixed. I'm not so concerned about any of that right now. You have other doctors working on those problems. I'm here today because I'm the ophthalmologist on staff. The eye doctor. You just might consider yourself lucky to be injured during these two weeks I'm on duty here."

Alex was becoming tense as he listened to the doctor.

"I'm gonna—live?"

"What's that? Live? Ah, sure—why not?" The doctor turned to the nurse beside him, lowering his voice: "Can he understand me?"

The patient raised his finger.

"I'm not going to kid you." Dr. Johnson expelled a weary sigh. "You've had a rough time, young man, but—uh, *Alex*—I'm sure you'll make a full recovery and be back to your usual self. It'll just take some time."

"You'll be back on your feet just as soon as you can," said Dr. Lindsay.

"How—long?"

"That's hard to say at this point," Dr. Lindsay responded. "Broken bones, usually six to eight weeks."

"Weeks?" Alex exclaimed as strongly as he could in his weak state. "I gotta go back—gotta find Eléna."

"Elaine?" asked Dr. Lindsay. "She's your…wife? …girlfriend?"

"She's…. I dunno…."

"He's faint," said Dr. Johnson.

Alex felt a hand fall lightly on his shoulder.

"I think you may have lost a good amount of blood, too," Dr. Lindsay spoke. "That's why you're probably feeling a bit dizzy. However, we've given you a transfusion."

"Yep, good ol' American blood," Dr. Johnson added, then went on. "Son, your bones are already healing nicely. They did a rather good job back in that clinic. Remember it? You were damn lucky they found you."

"I'm lucky…?"

"Now, I just need to check your eyes. Shall we proceed? Nurse, better hold your hand up to shield the light for him. That's good. All right, Alex. Ready?"

"Help—yourself—"

Alex sensed the nurse's hands blocking the light on his face. The doctor's pudgy fingers were tugging on his bandages. He felt the cold steel of scissors, the snipping of tape and gauze. Alex saw brilliant flashes of light that seemed to come from within his head, not from outside in the room. The dull ache that had pressed on his brain seemed to increase as the weight of the bandages was removed.

Suddenly a foul odor surrounded him. It seemed to fill the room. At that moment, he heard Dr. Johnson's sharp intake of breath, followed by "Oh my God...."

CHAPTER 11

"Here, look here," Alex had called to Eléna, walking on, pausing, walking and pausing. He was showing her he knew practically every nook and intersection just as it was described in the ancient poems. "By the layout of the walls here, we could be near the Treasury. That's where Priam kept the treasure of Ilium. The Achaeans took a lot of stuff back with them but it seems as though the Trojans hid most of it. Of course, later, that archeologist fellow, Schliemann, supposedly found some of it and gave pieces of the gold jewelry to his wife to show off for her society friends back in Germany. It might not be Troy number six, though, the city of Homer's tale, but one of the later cities built on top of it. The later villages never stayed for long. The bay was drying up, as I told you before."

She nodded, waiting for it to be over, and he appreciated her patience.

"Eléna, I'm actually here!" shouted Alex with the same enthusiasm he had shown on graduation day. "I feel like I've lived here before, you know. Like déjà-vu. I really think I was here long ago. Is that possible? What do you think, Eléna?"

"I think you read too many books," she responded, simply because he stopped to ask her. "That is why you feel that you have lived here. You lived and breathed this old myth for so long, Alex. You lived it all before in your books. You can get over it now."

"Get over it? This is the Holy Grail of my quest!"

She took his arm, gently at first, then, when he did not come with her, more strongly.

"Come, let us return now. It is hot."

Alex was staring hard at the landscape around him, the bright sun making him squint. The grasses were covered with dust and the fields were dried and brown. Alex could imagine an ancient day where men fought against each other over nothing. Only two of the warriors had any real squabble, he knew: Paris and Menelaus—followed soon after by Achilles and Hector, and all the others—but everyone was forced to wait out in the heat and dust and sun for the ten years it took to end it.

He regarded his lover. She appeared less sexy in her perspiration-stained blouse. She fanned herself, beads of sweat strung like pearls across the top of her bosom, matting her blouse where she had pressed against him. The war had lost its glory for her.

Eléna regarded him studying her. Suddenly she went to him, grabbed his shirt collar, and whirled him around, slamming him backward against the stone wall of the excavated building, slipping within the wall's protective shadow. With a quick glance in each direction and seeing no other tourists, Eléna slid her hands quickly down Alex's abdomen to his zipper as she pressed her lips against his. Her fingers unsnapped his pants.

He could not keep thoughts of their alcove sex in Hagia Sophia out of his mind—yet he felt differently now. He was standing in this most sacred of sites—sacred to him. He had spent a good portion of his life studying it and here he was, actually touching the stones, the dry Trojan air in his nostrils, his feet marking the same paths the Achaeans trod when they had ran madly through the midnight city slaying the drunken, sleeping Trojans. Whatever he held up as sacred, Eléna wanted to tear down, to profane. No, he thought, he had to draw the line somewhere.

"Not now," he said with a grunt.

He saw her frown, an artificial thing he knew was only an act.

"This is not the right time and place for making out."

"Don't you want to make love to me?" she said, adding a childish pout.

"Of course, I do. But here? In this public place? That's not right." He snapped his pants and swung his arm around her shoulders. "Besides, it'll be a lot better back in our hotel room, on the bed. Don't you think?"

"Come, the grass looks soft on that hill," she chanted, pointing.

Alex was unmoved: "Cut it out, Eléna."

"I want you, Alex." The woman breathed against his ear.

"Okay, okay," he laughed. "We can do that any time. Back at the hotel. We can do the sauna thing again, okay? Right now, we only have an hour or so to see everything else. And I *have* to see it all."

He stepped away from her as a new tour group, led by a uniformed woman carrying a small red and white flag, rounded the corner of the ancient street.

"And there were hot and cold springs," the guide narrated for her group of twelve, "like any city of that ancient time."

Alex grinned as the group brushed past him. Eléna corralled him in a loose embrace.

He broke from her arms and spoke in a raised voice over the guide: "*...where the wives of Troy and all their lovely daughters would wash their glistening robes in the old days, the days of peace before the sons of Achaea came.* Actually, the springs you're talking about are over there." He pointed in the opposite direction. "Didn't you read the book?"

At that instant, Alex noticed Eléna examining him in some strange but alluring manner: What did she see? A young man, innocent no longer, experienced in awkward fashions, perhaps? Her face shifted: less Helen of Troy and more Ellen of Illinois—as though she were realizing he was just a big bag of trivia, spouting importance like a fountain. He could see that reflected on her pastel face.

Alex glanced at his watch, decided to allot himself twenty more minutes.

"This is not what I want," Eléna announced.

Alex stopped. He spun around to face her. She stood, resting her hands on her hips, the six paces between them a no-man's land.

"What do you want?" he snapped.

"I want to leave this place. It's nothing but old stones

and dirt. There's not even a museum here to get out of the heat. I would rather make love with you, Alex—right here. In this dirty place—here, if you wish so much to stay among the ghosts."

"Eléna," he practically exclaimed, stepping toward her, "we don't have to make love in every historical site we visit!"

She stepped back, tripping on a stone but catching herself. She stood defiant before him—like Diomedes preparing to slaughter Trojans, he imagined.

"*You* came to *me*, yes?" she said.

Alex felt his world being split by an earthquake. He took several deep breaths. Clearly, the day was too hot and Eléna was tired of walking around.

"This is what I do," he said. "This is about history. It's all around us. It's the measure of humanity's efforts. It's the record of who we are, who we *were*. It's *everything*. For me, it is more than just a hobby or a casual interest. It's my life. You could call it my passion."

She hurriedly closed the gap between them and took his free hand in hers.

"Am I not your passion?" She patted his hand.

"Of course, you are," Alex responded, shifting his backpack in his other hand.

He saw something new in the corner of his eye, a feature he had not noticed before. Turning to study it, he saw what seemed like the burn marks of a torch on the stone wall. He stepped toward them, pulling as far as Eléna's arm would allow him.

"Just give me a few minutes more to really absorb it all,"

he said, pulling free from her to examine the stone wall more closely. "You should look at these, too, Eléna. You know that saying about history? That those who don't remember it are condemned to repeat it? It's true: what did humanity ever learn from this sorry episode? Better ways to kill each other?"

"You believe that?" Eléna asked, sternly. "Is that your fate talking to you?"

Alex glared at her. Her skin was shiny and moist. The sunlight reflected off her throat, almost blinding him. He realized his throat was dry. If only one of these dry basins were filled with water, he thought—but there was no rain in the Aegean between March and October—then he might take up her offer. They could shove each other into the pool, get completely soaked.

He caught himself: he was not some dog; he did not need to mark every place he visited with a sexual episode. And yet, the sight of Eléna's moist blouse distracted him from his archeological study—for a moment. He wanted to tear it off, wanted to see her breasts in the full sunlight.

No...patience, he commanded himself.

She grinned at him, slyly—perhaps planning, he decided.

No patience, Alex scolded himself, hearing his father's voice drift by on the dusty breeze. That would have to wait until they returned to the hotel in Çanakkale. They could shower, wash off the dust of Ilium, make themselves comfortable, and have the whole night to wrestle in the bed before returning to Istanbul.

He smiled at her, his pearly teeth glistening.

"Alex," she called, "shouldn't we go back and get something cold to drink?"

He did not hear her, lost in his lusty fixation.

"Alex?" She lowered her voice: "Do you hear me? I think it is time for me to go. I am too hot now, and I cannot find any relief."

He broke from his trance. "What did you say?"

However, he was still entranced by the ruins. She stared into his face again and he was three thousand years away.

"I am finished," said Eléna. "I am going back."

"Oh...," said Alex, not fully appreciating the way she had painted her voice in a slightly different, darker hue. "Okay, I'll meet you back where we started, at the gate."

He stepped off after the tour guide, several paces ahead, eager to take over the lecture.

"Good-bye, Alex," she called.

He glanced over his shoulder at her, as they moved in opposite directions, and shrugged off her lack of interest in the historical ramifications of the ruins of Ilium. All right, he thought, history wasn't her thing. Nevertheless, she should be able to understand and appreciate his interest in it. The polite thing to do was to let him enjoy it while he could. It wouldn't last forever. The buses would depart soon enough. They could do whatever she wanted to do when they arrived at the hotel.

After Ilium, thought Alex, catching up to the tour group, he and Eléna would return to their hotel room and he would make romantic, energetic love with her. A few more nights of such passion and their future life together would be set. He would wine and dine her in Istanbul and take her back to his home in California. He would show her his computer prowess, his video game creativity. More than games, it was to be his job. She would be impressed with his earning capacity, his ability to provide for her. And their children. They would have a good life together. His parents would fall in love with her, too.

CHAPTER 12

It was only twenty minutes, Alex suddenly recalled from his hospital bed. He was unable to sleep again. Only twenty minutes from the moment he first saw Eléna in trouble to the moment the police arrived to break up the fight. In his mind, he re-counted the steps across the site. He counted the heartbeats that had pounded in his head as he ran. A one-minute sprint. That was all it took to twist his life around full circle. Twenty minutes between having it all and losing it all—though there was still a chance of finding Eléna, he wanted to believe. If the unfortunate situation could not be corrected within seventy-two hours, he calculated, then it would leave a mark forever. It would result in a life as ruined as the ravaged, burned out husk of the lost city of Ilium.

With less than an hour before the tour buses were to head back, he hurried to see the remaining areas. It was more to soak up the ancient ambiance than to throw a virtual magnifying glass on any remaining stone carvings he might have missed. That ambiance had to last him until he returned home to California—or well beyond his return if he were to create a video game based on the war. It had to continue to inspire him after he began his new job in computer game design. Eléna was a big part of that. She was as much of the required ambiance as the hot, humid air and the weathered stones. In the twenty short minutes they were apart, he had ignored her, forgotten her, and everything was briefly and disastrously thrown back as it perhaps should have been.

Alex stood atop a buttress at the southwest corner of the site, peering out across the plain of Hisarlik, three thousand years earlier the harbor for Greek ships. Between there and the hill where stood the city of Ilium was the wide plain where most of the battles were fought. He tried to imagine the scene. As he scanned the site from his high vantage point, he saw groups of tourists being herded toward the entrance, back to the buses. Unattended children raced through the avenues. A couple here or there strolled casually. All the tour guide flags had been put away. He glanced at his watch, its alarm set so he would not miss the bus. That was Eléna's idea.

He smiled to himself and looked for her among the groups of tourists.

In the next neighborhood, as the Trojan streets were laid out, he thought he saw her: the flowing black mane, the voluptuous figure, the matted white blouse and fashion jeans. No doubt the woman was Eléna. No one looked like her, even from a distance. Up close, he mused, she was—

Three men walked near her. Turks, they appeared to be, and they gave his woman the once over as they passed her.

She turned, apparently at something they said. One of the Turks went to her as the two others held their ground, one crossing his arms over his chest, the other putting his hands roughly on his hips. What was happening? What did he say to her? She seemed defiant in her pose. The man spoke back to her, it seemed. The other two stepped forward. Alex saw them as an attack party about to pounce on his woman.

Alex hurried down the steps, what remained of them after so many years of warriors' and tourists' feet. He stumbled, caught himself and half-slid down the rest of the stones to the avenue below, loose stones following him.

He quickly ran through the city's streets and turned into the main plaza—probably the same place where the people of Ilium had pulled in their 'gift horse' from the Achaeans and partied around it late into the night. When they were all drunk or asleep, the thirty-two Greeks led by Odysseus opened the wooden horse's belly and slid down the rope to cut the victorious night loose from drunken reality. The slaying of warriors and women up and down every street, in and out of the homes and on every street corner, even in the sacred temples, forever stained the Greeks' triumph. They won the war yet they lost their honor.

Not much mattered about honor today, Alex decided, but he still felt some things had to be preserved at all costs, even paying the ultimate price. Patriot he was not, not so much as idealist—but even idealists got into the fighting spirit when hard times demanded action.

That reasoning rode fiercely at the front of his brain,

like a spearman on a charging chariot, as he rushed across the deserted plaza to save Eléna.

ꟷ

Reclined on his bed in the Navy clinic, Alex remembered getting the braces off his teeth years ago. He was glad his father, Brent Parris, D.D.S., timed the hideous braces to come off at fourteen, just the right age to begin using his new, perfect smile to his benefit in high school socializing.

"You always hear about the eyes being the windows to the soul, but that's not really true," his father had explained. "Open wider. Good. You can tell so much about a person's character by examining their teeth. But you know that already, right, son? Oral hygiene is a direct reflection of a person's morals. One more and we're all done. Hold on a minute, Alex. We choose to smile most of the time, and revealing our teeth is like opening our souls for inspection. I'm here to tell you, a person can lie with his eyes, but no one can fake a good set of teeth. Some try it with dentures, but I can spot even the best a mile away. Look at people's teeth, Alex, and you will know where they stand. Forget the eyes; eyes mean lies. Okay, done. Rinse and spit. And don't forget to smile."

Now it was Dr. Johnson's soothing voice he heard, but it was solemn. The man's relaxed yet confident baritone directed other voices in a medical discourse that could have been Turkish for all Alex knew. Hands probed his face, poked around his eyes, and seemed to caress his forehead and cheeks. The odor that surrounded him had rubbed itself into his nose. *Put the bandages back on*, he wanted to command them. A new vinegary, medicinal scent thankfully began to overwhelm the pungent one, making him nauseous. Some kind of disinfectant. The new odor meant that he and everything he could sense in the room was likely sterile.

"You're healing very nicely, Alex," said Dr. Johnson.

Alex sighed, imagining he was on his way home at last. He wanted to reach out for Eléna's hand, then he remembered that she had left him.

"Um…thank you…."

"Well, Alex, we've been examining you, as you no doubt have noticed. Doctor Lindsay is here, too. He's going to update you on some of your treatment options. I'll tell you, though, there's a problem with your eyes, and that's my specialty."

"What problem?"

"Yes, well, Alex. It seems as though…well, something that's not so good has happened to one of your eyes. Perhaps…uh…it must've happened during the fight you were in. Well, the cornea was cut. Cut open, in fact. Now, *that* can be repaired easily enough. We can stitch it back together and no one's the wiser. But…" and Dr. Johnson's voice trailed off.

"We suspect," Dr. Lindsay spoke up, "that the knife that cut your eye was probably the same knife that was used on your abdomen—which perforated your colon. The knife then slashed at your eyes. That's when your corneas were cut. Do you remember if you were stabbed in the abdomen first? More than likely that's where the infection came from. From your colon. A bit of fecal matter on the tip of the blade was enough to start a nasty chain reaction inside your eyeball—entering through the iris."

"Now, son," Dr. Johnson's voice returned, much too low and soft to be the bearer of bad news, "I'm afraid there's a much more serious situation that's developed."

"How serious?" asked Alex. "Am I going to have to wear glasses?"

Dr. Johnson chuckled uneasily.

"Not exactly, Alex. You see, what's happened is...well, there's an infection that's taken root there, like Doctor Lindsay told you. That's what you've been smelling when we remove your bandages. It's been rather aggressive. It's been eating away at the eyeball. Down inside the eyeball. It's...it's not likely you'll be able to recover your sight in that eye. There's just too much damage already."

"What do you mean?"

"The passage of light is going to be interrupted by the clouding caused by the infection as it passes through the eyeball. The eyeball is actually just a spherical gelatin mass that's basically transparent—"

"I know that!" Alex erupted. "You mean I can't see with that eye?"

There was a pause longer than he expected. Beneath the bandages, he listened for sighs, for shifts in heartbeats of the staff of doctors and interns in his room.

"You still there, Doc?"

"Yes, we're all here." It was Dr. Lindsay's cold voice.

"You had me worried."

"I'm the one who's worried, son." Dr. Johnson's voice

was no longer reassuring. "The damage to the eyeball is too great."

"How great?" asked Alex. "I mean, what do you *mean*?"

"Almost total destruction. You'll never be able to use it again," Dr. Johnson announced.

The room was silent and Alex could not even detect his own heartbeat.

Dr. Johnson cleared his throat. "Damn, I hate telling a young man this kind of news, but…son, what's more important now is the rest of your health. The infection is aggressive. It has not stopped spreading. It's continuing to eat away…there, inside…inside your head. Sure, you may not feel anything, but, believe me, it's doing its damage nevertheless."

"But I didn't do anything," said Alex. "It's not fair!"

"Son, I'm going to tell you straight out: we're going to have to remove it. Then we'll get to the infection."

Alex stopped thinking. His breathing stopped, then went into overdrive until a nurse took his hand and held it tightly.

"The eyeball. It has to come out," said Dr. Lindsay.

"Otherwise, son," said Dr. Johnson, "an aggressive infection like this one, you have to understand—well, it could get into your brain. Furthermore, that would be a disaster, son. There's no telling what kind of damage might occur. It might even prove...well, fatal."

Alex lay back against the up-raised bed, hearing the doctors and nurses slowly departing, leaving him alone with his thoughts. He wondered how so much had come to so little. It was only an eye, a glob of gelatin the size of a golf ball, a bunch of jelly, but so precious. He strained to calculate the actions he had taken in the past several days—ever since he was picked up on the side of the road—that might have caused this unfortunate turn of events. Somehow, he cursed, it must have been preventable. But how? By not going to Ilium? By not meeting Eléna? By not leaving California on this summer trip? Was he not good enough, not moral enough? Was it the trick of the gods? Had he insulted them? He was outraged.

The walls of his room fell away in a loud crash, the windows shattered, and he was hurtling like a rocket across the Turkish landscape in a nightmare he did not summon. Alex could not think, could not imagine this reality. He was always more comfortable in his archaic world where he knew the score. He needed to know how things would end before they began. And this adventure? He knew how it all would end: the siege of Troy and the long voyages home. There would Agamemnon be slain by his long-suffering wife, Clytemnestra, who had taken a lover during his long absence. There would Odysseus be forced to empty his house of his wife's lustful suitors. There would Menelaus return home with his adulterous Helen, to possess her again but never to trust her. There would Alex Parris, in so many ways like the son of Priam and brother to Hector, return to the sunny shores of California, as cruelly one-eyed as giant Polyphemus, the Cyclops blinded by Odysseus.

He smiled to himself, amused by the irony of his situation. With renewed strength, his laughter filled the room and soon brought a pair of nurses who increased the dosage of his pain medication. He choked, trying to hold back the angry tears. Tears! From the cavity where someday soon he would recall an eye had once been.

CHAPTER 13

He had only been defending Eléna, Alex told himself. It was his duty to protect her, to rescue her from the three Turkish men who were accosting her. When he saw her in peril from his higher viewpoint, he had charged down the slope and raced to save her.

"Hey, dude," one of three men he passed called after him, "where's the fire?"

"My girlfriend's in trouble!" Alex shouted back. "Over there!"

The young man, along with his two buddies, ran after Alex. They were off-duty U.S. Navy personnel, he found out later, sightseeing in civilian clothing. Shaking hands as they ran, Alex led the way into the plaza.

"Turks, again!" the one named Ruger snarled, seeing the situation. "Let's kick some Turk butt!"

"Hold on," the older sailor cautioned.

Alex approached the Turkish men: three tall, swarthy, mustached locals.

"What're you doing?" Alex shouted at them, catching them by surprise.

The three must have believed they were hidden from view, being behind the stone wall leading off the plaza. He quickly assessed the situation: the Turks were not frightened by his aggressive entrance and his military backup.

Eléna held her arm as if in pain, the blouse sleeve torn where one of the Turks had grabbed at her. It was easy to understand their attraction for her: the wet, matted blouse, the lacey bra showing through, her tight jeans accenting the curves of her hips. Alex saw a red mark on her elbow, certain that it was blood and not a smudge of the reddish soil.

"Save me, Alex," Eléna spoke. Her voice was weak, almost uncertain. It did not sound right, he thought in that instant. He could analyze it later, on the bus back to Çanakkale.

For now, his blood boiled into rage and he rushed into the trio of Turks. Taken by surprise, the first man was bowled over and the second came to help, throwing punches against Alex's ribs. The Navy men sprang into action and a group fistfight erupted, blazing among the stone blocks where Greeks had fought Trojans, in the very streets where the blood ran thick one night, millennia ago.

"Run, Eléna!" Alex cried out, taking a fist across his jaw and reeling.

He did not see where she went. Dodging the fist falls kept his eyes off her path of retreat. The fist in his gut left him breathless, but with a moment to recover—a gift of his compatriots who joined the fight—he stood and scanned the walls for her. He wound up his fists and began pummeling the man who had accosted Eléna. The Navy men took their cue from Alex and added their punches and kicks to villain number one. With every punch, Alex felt better; the fist strikes of the Turks had not wounded him. He was fighting for his woman. He was a hero.

Suddenly the local police arrived with whistles squealing and truncheons swinging, surrounding them. Alex and his friends let up. After all, they believed they were in the right and did not want to be seen as prolonging the fight. Instead, Alex and his new friends were the ones arrested.

The Turkish police officers, six or seven of them, knocked them to the ground and handcuffed them. Alex insisted that they were arresting the wrong people, that the three Turks had been molesting his girlfriend—a woman nowhere in sight now. It did not occur to him until later, in their jail cell where he had time to think, that probably none of the police officers understood English. If they had, then he would have been able to tell his side of the story, at least. It was just one big mistake, he knew. It would be straightened out soon enough and he could return to the hotel where his lady would be waiting for him.

From the clouds of dust that hovered over them, Alex saw the three Turkish men being ushered away—more like flies being shooed away, he considered. He and his fisticuff friends, the foreign troublemakers, were roughly herded out through Ilium's main entrance and shackled to the railing of the police truck's tailgate.

"I hope she got away," said Alex, seeing the last tour bus

pulling away and examining each window for a face he recognized.

"Who, your girl?" Chief Petty Officer Carter, the older one, asked.

"My girl…." Alex grinned, feeling that she was.

"Hey, Chief, this gonna be straightened out okay?" Seaman Benson, the youngest, asked his boss. "I gotta get back for my watch tomorrow morning."

"We'll talk about it later, Benson," Private First Class Ruger, the Marine, sneered, mocking his senior, CPO Carter.

"That's right," Carter confirmed sternly, his eyes narrowed to slits, aiming at his two junior charges. "You better plan on missing your watch. We'll discuss this incident when we get back to base."

"Wow," said Alex, "you guys are really going to be in trouble, aren't you? I mean, being Navy personnel, huh?"

Carter glared at him. "You and I won't be talking about this later."

"Thanks for your help, anyway," Alex offered.

"You should be."

They were hefted into the back of the flatbed truck like sacks of potatoes, still chained by their wrists to the railing. The truck drove away after some radio traffic by their police officers determined their destination: the town of Ezine, which had jurisdiction over the Ilium site. Alex knew it would all be over soon and he would be able to rejoin Eléna in their hotel in Çanakkale by the next day. Somewhere there was an embassy official who would be working all through the night to secure their release and smooth over this rather small international incident.

ꟸ

"Don't I get to make a phone call, too?" Alex had asked CPO Carter.

"Where do you think you are? Back on the block in Anytown, U.S.A.?" said Carter, chiding the civilian who started it all. "Don't worry. I took care of it."

"But they're a civilized country, aren't they?"

"Member of NATO, yes," PFC Ruger added, "but the lowest per capita gross domestic product of the whole organization. Barely made the cut. Got in on the third ballot. NATO keeps them around for the bases. Part of our orientation, and welcome to Turkey."

"Ruger, shut your stupid mouth!" Carter barked.

"If they've adopted European customs," said Alex, "then they should have the same basic principles of law, right? I *have* to make a call."

"Shhh! Here he comes," Benson muttered, seeing the shadow of their jailer rising up the wall as he approached their cell.

When the police truck had arrived, their jailer—he stood maybe seven feet tall and was beefy as a bull—stepped out of the small town constable station, hands on hips, and roared with delight. The idea of having four American troublemakers under his 'care' was better than a case of beer and an endless plate of shish kebab, Alex guessed. The big Turk constable seemed to make the most of his evening's entertainment, throwing each of them against the iron bars and slapping their faces back and forth for their crimes. He did not even seem to be asking any questions about what happened at Ilium. Alex protested, citing the Geneva Convention, and received a heartfelt punch to his stomach, which dropped him to the floor, leaving him gasping for breath. It did not take too much abuse for them to decide that they had to escape. Justice was not going to be served in this little country town, they realized.

Eventually, after shuffling through some stacks of papers, cleaning his pistol, and whistling some bawdy tune while he watched the foreign prisoners squirm, the constable left.

"He probably went out for dinner," said Carter.

"Dinner? At ten o'clock at night?" asked Benson.

"We need to make a plan. I'm not going to spend the night here, that's for damn sure," said Carter.

"Fuckin' A," said Ruger. "But what're we gonna do?"

They began making their plans.

When the constable finally returned, he bellowed his contentment, just for their annoyance. He stepped over to where the four of them were in the cell, five feet by five feet with no bench and no toilet. He said something, more to himself, apparently, as he paced the room, studying his captives, deciding how they could entertain him.

Another Turkish official entered the room bearing a tray covered with a towel. Raising the towel, they saw it was some kind of food. The constable and his deputy had a different idea: they sat down at the table and began eating the food themselves, going to great lengths to tease the prisoners. The big one held out his emptied plate for them to lick off if they were hungry, and laughed when no one took him up on his offer.

"Be patient," Carter instructed them. "We will get out of this. My wife should be here soon. With some payola."

"With what?" asked Alex.

"Money. A bribe, you know," Carter answered.

"Your wife's coming here?" Ruger asked Carter.

"We'll see. If she's still mad at me, we could be here a while."

"Why's she mad at you?"

"Oh, nothing serious," Carter sighed, obviously tired of explaining it. "Just a little affair I was having with the secretary. Some ensign's horny wife. Said she would forgive me but, hell, I still gotta live in the doghouse most of the time. What a bitch. Don't tell her I said that. You guys're so lucky you don't have a wife over here."

"You've done this before?" Alex asked. "I mean, buy your way out of trouble? Does it work?"

"You have to," Carter sneered. "It's the way things are done here." He studied the kid. "Sometimes it doesn't work."

CHAPTER 14

The woman who arrived at the jail had the appearance of a young girl dressed up to look older. In her short skirt and a low-cut blouse, 'Mrs. Carter' was obviously of Turkish ethnicity. She made an odd harem girl in her plastic baubles and beads. She still caught everyone's attention—above all, that of the constable. Beneath her heavy make-up and her moussed *faux* blondish hair, she seemed pretty. She sauntered into the constable station like some Hollywood diva, smiling at the Cyclops. He did nothing to hide his big toothy grin. Carter was clearly glad to see the woman arrive. Ruger had his eyes glued to her, until Carter pulled him off the bars.

She did a little dance, moving to music on the radio, and added exaggerated hip dips and breast jiggling that Alex thought was obscene. She opened her purse, almost as part of her dance, and as the constable looked inside at the roll of bills, she laid her arm across his wide shoulders. He did not seem to notice, counting the bills with his eyes. She made her simple request as her fingers walked circles around his back. When he did not get her idea, she went to plan B and handed him the roll of bills with one hand while pointing to the prisoners with the other hand. The Cyclops chuckled, a kind of 'you gotta be kidding' laugh and shook her arm off his back.

"She's giving you money, you dumb jerk!" Benson exclaimed, unnerved by confinement. "Just take it and let us go!"

Carter grabbed the boy and cupped a hand over his mouth, eyeing the woman. He gestured instructions to her. She sat herself up on the corner of the constable's desk and slowly slid her already short hem up her bare thigh. Everyone watched her.

"Where'd you meet *her*?" Alex asked Carter, the insinuation obvious.

"About a block off-base," Carter replied, not taking his eyes off the woman's seductive slow-dance. "In Izmir. She's really a nice girl. An orphan."

The constable was impressed, believing he was going to get lucky. Mrs. Carter took his hands and twirled him around like a dance partner. Alex conceded that the big man was indeed agile. Back in the United States, he thought, this Turkish giant could have had quite a distinguished career as a professional wrestler. The constable made no sudden moves, showed none of the viciousness he had demonstrated earlier. He was turning to putty in her hands, and as they danced he feigned kisses to her throat and she dipped just out of reach. Twirling around the room in his arms, she managed to whisk the key off the desk and over between the bars of the cell.

In the few seconds it took for the constable to notice,

entangled in the arms then legs of this saucy girl, Carter had the key in the lock and was turning it. The Cyclops tried to twist out of Mrs. Carter's grip but she held on tightly. Her full body weight hanging around the man's hips pulled him off balance and he tripped. Ruger grabbed the man's ankle through the bars and the constable toppled over like a giant redwood.

The constable crashed to the floor and the corner of the desk caught his temple as he fell, shoving his head sharply to one side.

"Ooo!" Mrs. Carter uttered, surprised.

"That's gotta hurt," Benson grunted.

"Holy shit! We knocked him out!" Ruger cried in disbelief.

"Well done, Sevâ," said CPO Carter.

The three Navy men pushed their way out of the cell with the constable's extended legs keeping the cell door from opening. They squeezed through and stood over the Cyclops.

"Is he dead?" asked Alex.

"No, just knocked unconscious," Carter announced. He went and hugged his rescuer, planting a kiss on her mouth. "Thanks for coming, Sevâ."

There was a trickle of blood on the constable's lips, though his face had hit nothing. Blood leaked from his nose, collecting in his thick moustache. Ruger quickly leaned over the body, fearlessly waiting for a breath.

"He's breathing." Ruger got up, shaking his head with satisfaction. "Nice job, uh, Missus Carter. If you really are the wife."

"Awright, she's not my wife," Carter barked, stepping over the constable's body. "But Sevâ treats me a helluva lot better. She got us outta here, didn't she? You better not say nothing, you hear me? Now let's get the hell outta here before the deputy returns."

"But shouldn't we get some medical help?" Alex asked the Navy men.

"What are you, some kinda ass-wipe?" Ruger sneered. "He didn't hit *you* very much, wimp. The bastard can go on and die for all I care!"

"Then it's murder," Alex reminded them, and for a second they paused.

"He's right. We need to...umm, hide him," Carter decided. "Let's move the desk over on top of him. That way, when the deputy returns, he'll think the desk fell on him."

"That's so lame," said Ruger. "Who's gonna think he pulled that big desk over on top of himself? Look. He wasn't even sitting in his chair."

"Yeah, who's gonna believe that?" Benson chirped.

"Just give me a hand," Carter ordered. "Now."

The four of them each took a corner and lifted the huge two-pedestal desk, each of them complaining how heavy it was, the drawers full and the top littered with papers which went flying across the room as they tried to carry the desk a few inches. Suddenly, as they were hovering over the constable's motionless body, their combined strength gave way and the desk slipped out of their hands. The constable's body erupted in a sharp groan.

"Oh, man!" Ruger almost laughed.

"You idiots!" Carter cursed. "How can you just drop the desk like that? Right on top of him! Now it's going to look intentional."

"He's bleeding now," said Alex, pointing to the constable's groin where one desk leg had planted itself.

"Now we really gotta get outta here," Carter shouted, brushing himself off and grabbing his wife's hand. "Come on, Sevâ."

"How we gonna get home, Chief?" Benson asked.

The door was swinging shut before Benson could get an answer or Alex could exit. The three of them ran as fast as they could in different directions, leaving Alex standing on the stoop in the darkness.

"Wait, guys!" Alex called after them.

He started down the steps but halted. Turning, he rushed back inside and frantically searched through the mess of papers on the desktop. There it is, he sighed: his passport!

Outside again, Alex saw Benson jogging down the street, and then turned into an alley. Alex shoved his passport in his back pocket and quickly followed, leaving the burly Cyclops on the floor of the station with the desk positioned atop his body. He had a small speck of satisfaction that no murder had been committed. A return of brutality he could live with, but all of the digitized blood that he regularly saw spewing from various wounds on video victims was nothing compared to the growing puddle of dark liquid radiating outward from the Cyclops' head and groin.

"Benson! Wait!" Alex yelled, momentarily forgetting the

art of stealth.

It was late enough that the townsfolk were shut in their homes for the night. Most of the homes were dark and only the occasional street lamp showed him the maze of narrow stone streets he had to negotiate.

"Where's Carter?" Alex asked the junior sailor when he caught up with him in the shadows of the alley, hiding from a late-night shopkeeper heading home.

In the lamp's glow, they saw a blue and white taxi settled against the opposite curb. Its doors were closing. It was CPO Carter and his Turkish mistress.

"There he is," Benson growled, pointing.

They jogged up to the side of the taxi and tapped on the window. The driver waved him off, concerned about the customers he already had.

"Carter, wait!" Alex called through the window. "We have to wait for Ruger."

The CPO shook his head slowly, rolled the window down a crack.

"Why don't you guys take another cab home, huh? Me and Sevâ wanna have some time alone. It's two hours or so back to Izmir and we need that time. You know, for me to thank her, and…well, you understand."

"Yes, I understand," said Alex. He looked inside at the gaudily dressed woman grinning back at him. Maybe she wasn't that pretty, after all.

He stepped back from the vehicle and the taxi pulled away from the curb, made a U-turn in the street and roared off. He and Benson could only wave goodbye at Carter and his girlfriend, already locked in a tight embrace in the back window as the car drove away. They watched the tail lights fade, listening to the crickets and the rustling of the dark trees that lined the street.

Benson suddenly jerked Alex from his trance with a gesture to get into the shadows. A motorcyclist whizzed past them. They stepped back into the street.

"Any other taxis?" asked Alex, thinking that was probably the last one.

"Benson!" a voice called. It was Ruger, jogging down the street in the direction Carter had left. He found their hiding place in the alley and ducked in.

"The Chief left us on our own—just like I knew he would," Benson explained. "He and his 'wife' took the last taxi for themselves. Now we gotta hitch a ride."

"Figures, that asshole," Ruger sneered.

"Where'd *you* go?" Alex asked Ruger and the Marine threw a thumb behind him. Alex saw his knapsack. "Hey, that's my bag!"

"I went back to get our stuff," he said, proudly, lifting Alex's knapsack off his shoulder. "And fix that freakin' bastard once and for all. He ain't gonna be beating up nobody else!"

"Quiet," Alex cautioned them. They each glanced in a different direction. The town was shut up for the night.

"What'd you do?" asked Benson, his voice lowered. His eyes widened as Ruger displayed his collection of items. "You kill him?"

"No, fool," Ruger snapped at his sidekick. "I shoulda, though." He counted off some Turkish lira and handed them to Benson. "Here's yours. But I did lift up the desk, the corner anyways, and let it slam back down on his head. Here, take this watch."

"You didn't!" Alex exclaimed, then hushed himself in the echoing street.

"Did. You need some? Here, dude." Ruger handed Alex a few bills. "He was breathing when I left, though."

Alex hated the Marine's attitude but he could not bring himself to say anything. They had helped him. They were in trouble because they helped him. Now they were in it together, no matter what would happen next.

Ruger produced more souvenirs from the knapsack.

"From the fat bastard," Ruger explained, examining a shiny penknife and slipping it into his own pocket. He reached into the bag again. "How about this pipe thing? Kinda neat, huh?"

"I suppose so," said Alex, and took a deep breath, surrendering to his fate. The gods had decreed that he spend the night with these two uncouth strangers. He thought perhaps it was the punishment that fit his crime: talking too much about nothing important.

Ruger reached into the knapsack, then stretched his hand toward Alex. "Here. Present for you."

"What's that?" asked Alex, and Ruger opened his hand to reveal a black leather wallet.

"Take it."

"What? You took the man's billfold?" Alex threw his hands into the air in disbelief. He paced around them. "Assault, now larceny? What were you thinking?"

Ruger snapped the wallet at Alex, who reacted in time, catching it against his chest. Alex glared at the Marine, then opened the wallet. Inside were several plastic sleeves containing photos.

"Pictures of his family," said Alex. "He's got a family. A son and two daughters. He's just a policeman doing his job. And we've killed him."

"Don't be so fucking soft," growled Ruger. "He's a sadistic bastard."

"He got what he deserved," said Benson.

"They have to be maybe seven and ten years old, the girls," Alex mumbled, "like my cousins. The boy must be about twelve. He looks like his dad. And here: here's the wife." He showed the picture to Ruger, who turned away.

Benson leaned in for a look. "Ugly woman, ain't she?"

"That's a nice thing to say." Alex studied the wide, flat cheeks and small, dark eyes, the double chin and limp, black hair of Mrs. Constable. "But she's *his* woman, at least." He tried not to think of Eléna. He closed the wallet. "So what am I supposed to do with this?"

"Keep it," said Ruger. "It's a souvenir."

"I don't need anything to remind me of this place," said Alex, looking over at Benson.

Benson was staring at a white ceramic cylinder, open on one end, and slightly wider at its closed end, carved with figurines of exotic ballerinas along its four-inch length. "Cool! What is it?"

"I think it must be some kinda sex thing. See these girls here?"

"Look—what's that?" Benson pointed to the two knobs on one side.

"That must be for—"

"That's where the handle broke off," said Alex with derision. "It's a stupid coffee mug."

Ruger and Benson stared at it from all sides.

"Or it's a bong," said Alex with a sigh. His roommate had one displayed on the desk in their dorm room, he recalled, like the water pipe was some grand symbol of defiance against authority. It was never used during the time they shared the room.

"Yeah, looks like you're right," Ruger chuckled. "I'll keep it anyway. For a souvenir. Here, hold it for me." He thrust it at Benson.

"We already crushed his pelvis the first time with the desk," Alex reminded them. "And you steal the things on his desk, too?"

"Pelvis," Benson snickered and told a joke about Elvis Presley.

"Very funny," Ruger groaned.

"After crushing his pelvis, we were in big trouble," Alex announced, glaring at Ruger. "Now you go *back* and drop the desk on his *head*? I don't know, but you *really* deserve some kind of punishment. You're some kind of a maniac, Ruger! Don't you have any sense of morality?"

"I said he was breathing, moaning even, when I left," said Ruger, slinging the knapsack onto his shoulder. "He'll just have one freakin' fat headache in the morning."

"It'll be morning soon enough," said Alex. "Let's just...just get going. Out of this town. That's the first thing we need to do. And fast."

They agreed, stepping off at a leisurely gait down the street, headed in the direction Carter's taxi had gone, and quickly fell into a brisk march.

"And then where?" Benson whined every time they reached an intersection. "How are we gonna get back? I'm already gonna miss my watch. I gotta be there at o-six-hundred. They're gonna kill me."

"Stop saying 'kill', you two!" Alex snapped.

"Look at this," Ruger commanded. When they looked, he showed them one more souvenir: the constable's black eye patch. He looked at Alex. "Want it?"

Alex frowned. "What do I need an eye patch for?"

"You can be a pirate," said Benson.

"No, Alex replied, "but it might make an interesting video game. I mean, sailing the seven seas and all. That's my line of work: designing video games."

"Cool," said Benson.

"I also cut off his fuckin' moustache with a pair of scissors," Ruger said. "He's gonna be so freaked, he ain't never gonna mess with nobody never again. Bet it took him, like, ten years to grow that thing."

"Ruger, you are sick." Alex shook his head in disbelief, thinking of at least two of his frat brothers who were carbon copies of this wayward Marine.

Ruger feigned anger, then chose to take it as a compliment and began laughing.

"I give it to you, fearless leader, the idiot that got us in this fucked up situation! It'll look great on you. You can be a pirate or something."

"That's what I said," Benson piped up.

Alex halted as the other two continued on a few paces before stopping and looking back at him.

"Come on," said Ruger.

"Wait a minute," Alex thought aloud. "Did you get your papers or ID cards? How about my camera? I was in too much hurry to get them, but I found my passport, at least."

Ruger's face went blank. "Aaa, you don't need that stuff...do you?"

"You don't need your IDs?" asked Alex.

"I sure need *mine*!" said Benson.

"Oh, I am *so glad* I left my really important things back in the hotel—like my plane ticket. I need to find a phone and call the hotel, and tell them to extend my reservation. My backpack needs a room for the night. Dad's gonna go crazy."

"Hotel? Hah," Ruger laughed. "What a pussy!"

Benson snickered. "Swimming pools, movie stars."

"And my camera. I had a dozen rolls of film shot."

"You can buy a picture book of the place, you know," said Benson. "I saw them at the souvenir stand."

"Shut up," Ruger growled at Benson.

"Well, I sure hope we don't get stopped," said Alex. "What about your ID cards? Do you think they'll just toss them in the trash when they find the Cyclops dead? No, they're going to be looking for you. At least I didn't do anything."

"You didn't do anything? You started all this crap!" Ruger cursed.

"Yeah, you started it," Benson concurred.

They argued about the episode for another mile.

"Well, he ain't dead," Ruger insisted.

"He could be by now," said Alex.

Benson motioned them off the road and they stepped into the shadows of the trees as a vehicle drove by.

"What're we gonna do?" Benson whined as they all agreed to jog on through the streets and get away from the station. "I got my watch in an hour!"

"Will you shut your mouth?" Ruger exploded. "You've been saying that for six hours! You're not going to make it back in time, so just shut up already!"

"Oh, take it easy," Alex cautioned.

Ruger quickly feigned a slap to his head. "You sure don't get a pass, neither."

CHAPTER 15

By the time the sky was turning orange along the horizon of jagged hills, Ruger found a sign giving directions to Izmir. Once they were clear of the town they had slowed to a walk, breathing heavily as the road wound up and down the hills, bending and twisting through the rugged terrain.

"I need to get back to Çanakkale," said Alex, trying to catch his breath. "My girlfriend's waiting for me…and if I don't show up, well…you know…."

"Know what?" Ruger asked. "She's gonna be pissed, so what? Let her deal with it. That's what bitches do."

"She's not like that," said Alex.

Ruger glanced at him. "What's your name again? Parris? Oh, yeah—like freakin' Parris Island, U.S. Marine Corps training facility. Hoo-rah!"

"Excuse me," said Benson, "we gotta figure out a way to get back to base. Got any ideas where we are? And how to get on the right road?"

"Ain't got a clue," Ruger said with a shrug.

Ruger seemed to have no concern for being AWOL or being on the run from the Turkish authorities. This was part of the adventure for the young Marine, thought Alex. Benson was happy to follow wherever they went. They had lost the directions for Izmir and decided to go cross-country to avoid any police traffic on the main road. The darkness and the uneven terrain made their progress slow.

"I think we've been going inland, for the most part," Alex explained, sticking his wet fingertip in the air. The others watched curiously. "The sea's that way," he said, pointing his finger in the opposite direction they had been going for the past two hours.

Dawn was creeping over the hills in front of them.

"That's east, guys," Alex declared. "The coast is south and west of us, I remember from the map. We've been heading inland, like I said. We're going parallel to the coast now. We need to turn south now, or turn to the right. Starboard, for you sailors, huh? That should take us to the coast."

"That's the same way we came. This here's the only road," said Ruger.

"When we get to the coast, I'll head north back to Ilium and you guys can go south to Izmir," Alex suggested, ignoring Ruger.

Alex did not have a sense of direction either, lost in a dusty countryside now in the dawn light. All the signs they had passed were in Turkish and they naturally avoided anybody they could have asked for help. They really were on their own.

He paused at the top of the next ridge to contemplate the sunrise, the salty sea breeze blowing inland to them.

He stood tall, there on the prow of the ship.... The battle had been fought, won even. Finally, after ten bloody years. Now they were sailing back from vanquished Ilium, trying to reach home. Alex pondered the fate of Odysseus as they stepped down the side of the ridge they had just mounted, winding their way through the brush and ditches. He impressed the military guys with his sense of geography, and in the morning light they saw he was correct after all and followed him.

Ruger broke out laughing suddenly as they walked down a gravel road to nowhere.

Alex asked what was so funny.

"Really kicked some Turk butt, didn't we?"

Benson smiled, ready to laugh with Ruger but taking his cue from Alex.

"You know, Private Ruger—" Alex began.

"That's Private First-Class Ruger!" and the Marine *hoo-rah*ed.

"PFC Ruger," Alex continued. "You remind me of Achilles. You both have the same attitude."

"Who you talking about?"

"Achilles. The Greeks' hero at Ilium. The Trojan War? Remember, we were there just yesterday, where it all happened thousands of years ago. Achilles was strong and fearless, sorta like you, but he was also stubborn and petty."

"What do you mean by that?"

"I mean, he was stupid. Like in an IQ test way."

"You calling me stupid?" and Ruger threw a fist at Alex, who stepped back. "Let me tell you a thing or two, college boy. I know a lot about being a Marine. Helluva lot! You couldn't never take apart no M-60 machine gun and put it back together again, all with your eyes closed. In three minutes flat, too. Then shoot bull's eyes in a row of thousand meter targets in one minute flat. *You* couldn't do that!"

Alex chuckled. "Why would I want to?"

Ruger straightened up, red faced with anger, and launched his foot into the air at the civilian: Tae Kwan Do kick or such, Alex guessed. His dirty shoe just grazed Alex's shoulder, but it was enough to cause him to stumble backward and lose his balance.

"You're the stupid one, ya freak!" said Ruger.

"Hey, guys," Benson intervened.

"All right, all right." Alex picked himself up. "I said Achilles was a great fighter, the darling of the Achaeans. He was famous…the most famous warrior on the Greeks' side. And very devoted to his mother. He had a boyfriend, too: his cousin, Patroclus, who was slightly older and was eventually killed while wearing Achilles' armor. You see, Ruger, I've studied all of it for years. I came here to see it for myself, and to feel it, and breathe in the air. I know it sounds strange to someone like you, but that's my reason for being here. For you, however…well, it must be your fate. Anyway, Achilles had only one weakness: his heel."

"His heel?" Ruger exclaimed. "Now *that's* what's stupid!"

Alex led them along a wood slat fence, separating the wild fields from an olive grove. Seeing a broken slat ahead, they decided to cross there.

"Why didn't he wear any boots," Benson asked, "you know, to cover his heels?"

"Because if he did, then we couldn't call them Achilles heels," Alex explained.

They stared at Alex a moment.

"See, his mother was a sea nymph named Thetis," Alex continued, "and when Achilles was born she wanted to protect him and make him strong, so she held him by his heel and dipped him in the River Styx—which dead warriors had to cross to enter Hades—and that made him tough, but his heel didn't get in the waters—"

"Another freakin' story by the Greeky boy," said Ruger and laughed.

"During the war, Achilles was killed by an arrow that struck his heel."

"Man, you can't die from a wound to your heel like that."

"You could if the arrow was poisoned." Alex shook his head. "It's just a story, Ruger. He did die. That's a fact, or as much of a fact as anybody can prove."

"Why'd they aim at his heel, anyway?" Benson asked Alex.

"I doubt that anyone was aiming at his heel," Alex explained, "the arrow just went there." He thought for a heartbeat, knowing what came next but holding back.

"Then what happened?" asked Benson. "Who shot him?"

"Uh…well, Achilles was killed by the arrow that was shot by Paris. The guy who was Helen's lover. You know, the young prince of Ilium."

"By Paris?" Benson snorted in laughter, realizing the

irony.

"Close," said Alex, hiding his smile.

Benson tripped over a fallen fence slat and the other two broke into laughter as he picked himself up, noticing the goat dung staining his pants.

"Watch where you're falling, huh?" Alex chuckled.

Ruger sneered: "You mean, Parris, the suburban whiz kid wimp from California kills the street-tough warrior Achilles from Big D Texas?"

"It's just a story."

"You're making this up, aren't you?"

"No, it was made up long, long ago by a blind poet named Homer. As a matter of fact, he was born in Izmir. Probably not far from your Navy base. How's that for coincidence?"

"You're full of shit, Parris," Ruger growled. "Blind poet…shit, man. That bastard sheriff back there must've walloped you good 'longside your head."

"All I was saying was that you remind me of Achilles," said Alex, almost tripping over a stone partially hidden in the grass. "He was brave and strong, yes, but he didn't have any thoughts in his head other than beating up somebody. All he was good at was fighting. He wasn't even particularly good at leading men. Too stubborn and petty. He was great only at hand-to-hand combat."

"Sounds like my kinda dude," Ruger chuckled, giving Benson a knowing slap on the back. "How about you? You into that fighting stuff?"

"Me? The Navy's gonna pay for my college in a couple of years," said Benson. "I'm gonna be studying electrical engineering, going for the big bucks. Sure don't know why I ended up here, though. They promised me I could see Europe."

"And they sent you to Turkey?" Alex grinned. "Cheer up. It's almost Europe. A guy I knew in college, in my fraternity, he joined the Navy and asked for Europe. They sent him all the way to Newfoundland."

"Where's that?" Benson asked.

"Off the coast of Canada. North of Boston," Alex replied. "They must've thought that was part of Europe."

"So you're a college dude, huh?" Ruger jeered.

"Graduated last May," Alex said. His chest seemed to puff out a little as they marched through the morning.

"So what the hell're you doing over here?" asked Ruger after a moment.

Alex did not answer, surveying the hillside ahead of them and deciding it was not the right direction.

"Hey," Ruger shouted. "I asked you a question."

"He wants to know what's your excuse for being here," Benson repeated.

Alex stopped hiking, wiped his brow and sighed.

"I came to conquer Ilium," said Alex with unexpected boldness. "Let's take a rest here for a couple minutes, okay? We can pick some olives for lunch. They look ripe enough."

Benson produced the beverage can Ruger had swiped from the constable's station: canned black coffee, they discovered, now warm and bitter. They passed it around until it was empty. Benson crushed it against a stone and slipped it in his hip pocket.

"For a souvenir," he joked.

Ruger flopped down in the grass after checking it for goat piles.

"Hey, Parris!" the Marine called, but Alex was lost in his own thoughts.

Alex lay back against a fence post, gazing up at the blue sky and its fluffy, innocent clouds. He wondered if Eléna was looking at the same clouds from wherever she happened to be. He wondered if she was thinking of him. The warm sun soothed the soreness from his all-night hike. With his belly trying to digest a handful of hard, bitter olives, his mind grew dull, sleepy, but he refused to give in.

What did he always say? He came to conquer Ilium? He realized he must be exhausted to say something so abstruse. *Abstruse? There I go again.* Yet he did come to conquer Ilium, he had to confess. He came to steal its secrets—its secret treasures. When he arrived, he saw there was nothing worth taking. A few photos maybe, but nothing of value. It had already been looted by the tourist trade. He came to conquer and found Ilium already ravaged. Where did that leave him? He could return home claiming victory, an easy rout of an already-vanquished foe, or he could explain that he only came for the sights. Now, he realized, he was running away from the battleground.

Alex turned back to the Marine.

"We're all in this together, you know," he started. "If I can't lead you back home, wherever that is for you, then I won't be able to reach home myself. It's all tied together."

"I thought I was in command here," Ruger snorted.

"No, Ruger," Alex spoke firmly. *Because you're a fool,* he added in thought. "Come on, we'd better get moving again."

They stood and stretched. Alex, dressed for a hike and wearing boots, set the pace as Ruger and Benson followed, wearing sneakers.

"So I came as Agamemnon," Alex mumbled to himself, "to reluctantly serve my curiosity and now I'm cast adrift like the Poseidon-baiting Odysseus."

"You say something, Parris?" the Marine called.

Alex glared at him, Odysseus to Achilles. "Just thinking."

After Ilium

CHAPTER 16

Eléna would be worried about him, thought Alex. She must be trying to get in touch with Turkish authorities to track him down. She would know what to do. He just needed to get to a place where he could be found. Seeing him fighting for her, she would have worried about him all the way back to the hotel. She would have contacted the U.S. embassy in Istanbul. Even now, an elite team of rescuers were combing the coastal hills for a trio of wandering fools. Any moment a helicopter would swoop down on them and they would be saved. Alex grinned. She cared for him. Maybe not so much the way he was carrying on at Ilium, but before that, certainly. If their relationship was to grow, they would have to look beyond one bad day. Already he was thinking how to summarize his adventure for their grandchildren.

First, he had to be found. Traipsing through the wild terrain was not such a good place. If he could get to a telephone or, better yet, a computer hooked up to the Internet, he would contact Eléna. He could send an e-mail to the embassy, too. At the least, he considered, tourist hotels would have internet for making reservations, right? He looked around the countryside, unable to feel confident about an internet connection even in the next village they might find. Most importantly, he needed to reassure her that he still loved her. He couldn't risk leaving her with that last, bad impression: Alex as a boring historian.

Everything he did now was for Eléna.

"Well, looky here," Ruger announced.

They were cutting through abandoned farmland and had entered a secluded meadow, bordered on each side by scrub brush and by a small grove of trees on a third side.

"Did you find a phone?" asked Alex with deliberate sarcasm.

"Nope, it's dope."

"Oh, you mean 'mary-*hwan*na'?" Benson inquired, mocking him with slurred speech.

Ruger laughed. "Man, *you* never tried any, I'll bet," he teased Benson.

"In school, sure did," the young sailor boasted. "Every weekend, just about." He turned to Alex, gesturing.

"No, not me," Alex confessed. "Some of my fraternity did. Mostly they all preferred beer. Is this really...? What makes you sure this is marijuana?"

"I know what it looks like, man," said Ruger. "My brother used to grow it in his backyard, in secret, like. Had some in his basement, too, growing under some heat lamps. Over here, this ain't the cheap stuff. Looks wild. Maybe this is real hashish. Premium shit."

"No way," said Benson.

Ruger laughed. "We hafta try it."

"Looks like a bunch of dried up old weeds," said Alex.

"It's *weed*," Benson laughed.

"Growing wild," Ruger continued. "Or it's supposed to *look* like it's growing wild, like something natural out in this field. Nobody's planted it, it just grows wild, yeah. We'd better keep a lookout for whoever's growing it. They'll still be keeping an eye on it."

"Ruger," Alex barked to get his attention, "this is Turkey! It's still illegal. They don't grow it for recreational purposes. It's more illegal here than in the U.S. Didn't you see that movie? You can get in serious trouble with that stuff!"

"*Midnight Express*!" Benson exclaimed. "That's it. Saw it six times. You oughta see it while you're stoned."

"Relax, you ass-wipes," said Ruger. He stepped to the edge of the field and took a stalk in his hands, examining it. He crumbled some of the leaves into powder. "It's so dry here all the leaves are shriveled up. Sun-dried hashish. We could probably smoke it right now."

"With what?" asked Benson, taking a look at the plants. "We don't have any paper to roll it in. No lighter or matches."

"College boy's got a lighter," Ruger responded.

"It's Carter's," Alex explained. "I only picked it up when he ran out of the jail. I don't even smoke."

"So you won't mind handing it over," said Ruger with a sneer. "I been dying for a smoke ever since we got picked up."

Ruger and Benson began stripping the dried leaves off several stems with more enthusiasm than they had shown with the olives.

Alex took the opportunity to sit down in the grass and pull off his boots. His feet were sore and blistered. He had not planned on a long hike when he got dressed the previous morning for a simple bus trip to Ilium.

Lying back, he watched the clouds pass overhead. He cocked his arms back under his head and stared up at the sky as his bare feet breathed.

Like their hotel in Istanbul, the hotel in Çanakkale had a sauna—what they naturally called the Turkish baths. He had wondered if they could make use of it like they had the one in Istanbul. The sauna was segregated, of course, but late at night Eléna had sneaked him into the women's side, thinking that all good and proper women would be up in their rooms while the men would gladly sit in their side of the sauna late into the evening. He and Eléna had remained alone there, sweating profusely, and soon were embraced, united in their merging streams of moisture. Alex relaxed as he thought back, remembering how the baths were too hot for him to become aroused. His heart beat rapidly and he thought he was going to pass out. Eléna had assured him he would be all right and lowered the temperature dial. Not so traditional, he laughed, using natural gas instead of hot rocks and water.

"What're you cracked up about?" Ruger asked.

"Thinking back, that's all," Alex replied. "Eléna and I went to this sauna in the hotel in Istanbul, and we—"

"Yeah, okay, that's enough," Ruger snapped.

Had he really been talking about Eléna so much?

"You've been talking about that woman all night and all

morning. Give it a rest," Benson growled. "Who is she, anyway—your big sister?"

"Big sister!" Ruger snickered. "Yeah, she *was* kinda old. A little on the, umm, chubby side, too. You can pinch an inch of *her*. How'd you hook up with her, anyhow? Man, those skinny-ass blondes, that's what I go for."

"Me, too," Benson said with a sigh. He launched into a dialogue with Ruger about which models and TV stars they liked and which ones they wanted to—

Alex wanted to protest their presumptions about Eléna. He explained how they met, about the coincidence of their names. Eléna was not chubby; her body was 'voluptuous', a word they would never have understood: full-bodied, womanly, not skinny like some teenager. He was proud of the way she looked; he was aroused by her. She wasn't that much older, certainly not old enough to be losing her beauty.

He decided to ignore them. Who was this woman? he wondered, taking on their narrow frame of mind. The cause of their present circumstances, that's all they knew of her. They saw that she was older than he was. Maybe they did not find her so attractive, he thought. Maybe she was only *his* hang-up. Who was she? Eléna was his girlfriend, he decided. His paramour, his heart shouted back. The difference was a matter of time: the former promising a future, the latter limited to the present.

He was about to announce his conclusion when Ruger slapped his shoulder.

"Here, try this," offered the Marine.

It had taken the two of them an hour to construct

something with which to lose their minds, Alex noted. He had almost fallen asleep in the grass while they worked. Benson had fashioned the crushed beverage can they had emptied earlier into a tray. They set the tray inside the coffee mug. Benson crumbled dried leaves and made a pile on the flattened can. Ruger carefully lit it with Carter's lighter. Soon the smoke rose in a slow swirl out of the mug. Ruger and Benson stood close, closer than real men would ever stand to each other, and brought the smoking mug up to their faces, in turn. Without the filtering effect of water, this reinvented hookah gave them stronger hits—so Ruger said. They sucked the acrid smoke deep into their lungs and held it as long as they could.

"You guys aren't going to be any use to anyone now," said Alex. "We *need* to keep on the move, and get to someplace where we can get help." They ignored him, as he expected. "I should *never* have taken up with you guys. We should've split up back in the town. We're going in opposite directions anyway."

"Ain't you supposed to be our leader?" Ruger laughed.

Benson echoed the laughter, then, "Yeah, give us an order."

"Just see what happens, huh?" added Ruger.

Comfortable in the grass, ready to nap after the all-night hike, Alex casually observed his two companions' downward spiral.

"I don't know why you guys think you need to do that," said Alex.

"Cuz it's here," Ruger told him, holding his breath and cupping the smoke toward his face. "Never get any back on base."

Benson snickered in delight.

"Just like that goat dung we stepped in last night," Alex chuckled.

"But this is good shit." said Benson, holding in the smoke. He finally exhaled. "You gonna try some?"

"No, thanks, guys. I'm usually the designated driver. Somebody's got to keep straight. I'd better be the one to try to figure out a way home."

"Man, what *is* it with you, anyway?" cursed Ruger on half air rations. "You are so freakin' establishment. You been acting crazy since we met, all flaky with the Greek Wars and all. I mean, what the hell you talking about, all this crap about Trojans? All your freaky Greeky talk? *Man*, you need some of this hash *real* bad, dude!"

Alex sat up, leaned back on his outstretched arms.

"You want to know about the Trojan War, huh? Okay, I'll tell you. You guys have heard of Odysseus, haven't you?"

"No. Who's that?" asked Benson.

"How about Ulysses? Same as Odysseus."

"Okay, heard of Ulysses."

"You mean General Grant?" Ruger asked.

Alex shook his head wearily.

"Don't mind him. He's a war freak," Benson explained, growing red faced behind the smoke. "Loves everything about wars, the Civil War especially."

"The Civil War?" Alex checked. "That figures, you being such a hawk."

"Yeah, like a hawk," Ruger agreed. "You know...The!

Civil! War!"

"Which one?"

"What the hell you mean, which one? North and South. Blue and Gray. You're *probably* one of them damn Commies."

"Well, as you *probably* know, the British had a civil war in the sixteen-hundreds," Alex lectured to his stoned students. "The French had one in seventeen-eighty-nine—well, most people call it a revolution. The Russians had one, too. In nineteen-seventeen, the Bolsheviks took power and other groups wanted to stop them. Civil War. The Bolsheviks won, and you know them today as your so-called Commies. Even those stubborn *Americans* had a civil war. Yugoslavia's got one going on now—again. It's nineteen-ninety-three and we still have civil wars! Everybody has civil wars. They give us historians something to write about. It's either civil wars or world wars. Or revolutions. Take your pick. It's got to have some drama. Nobody's interested in reading about troubled lovers in history."

"Oh." Ruger was puzzled. "I thought it was just the name of the war. That's all I ever heard it called."

"Not the 'War Between the States'?"

"I heard that name before," Benson joined in.

"It's not so accurate, though." Alex realized that he enjoyed playing mind games with these two. "It should be the 'war between two groups of states'. It wasn't every state for itself. Don't you know what 'civil' means, Ruger?"

"I'll take Trojan War for five hundred, Alex," said Benson.

"And remember to put your answer in the form of a question," Alex played along.

"What's the Trojan War got to do with guys lost in Turkey?" Benson continued, much to Alex's sudden chagrin.

"There are Greeks," Alex responded as he waited for Ruger to focus, "and there are Greek organizations."

"Don't it mean like to get along?" Ruger offered.

"Like 'let's all be civil now,'" Benson added.

Ruger slapped at Benson, who fell over in the grass, laughing loudly.

"Yes, that's it, PFC Ruger," Alex cheered. "It's all about getting along. Whenever anybody says 'let's be civil,' it usually starts wars. You're on to something, now. Better write this down, it could be important. Our story begins with Odysseus, also known as *Ulysses*—not the Union general in the American Civil War but the king of Ithaca, an island on the western coast of Greece...."

As he recited the old tale, Alex watched his comrades reclining in the smoky grass, yapping at each other and singing something that sounded to him like the Marine's Hymn. He told them the story of Odysseus. They were not listening, of course, but he no longer cared. It was a way to pass the time. The storytelling was for him. He needed it to keep his adventure grounded in reality; if he could compare his adventure to a story, then things weren't too bad.

"Hey, PFC Ruger," Alex called. "Bet you can't do your machine gun trick *now*!"

"Say *what*?" the drowsy Marine responded.

With a sly grin playing on his face, Alex reflected on his newly appointed position as captain and chief lecturer to these two junior warriors. His fraternity brothers had all been taller, stronger, more athletic, drove faster cars, got more girls, but he had always felt smarter than any of them. Alex couldn't be sure if he really was. He certainly was the older, wiser man now.

That same sense of superiority drove him to stand up at the unexpected engine noise, questioning his hearing. Was it thunder, or was he confused by their boisterous laughter? He waved at his comrades to quiet down so he could listen better and only then noticed that the field itself was smoldering. Although he could see no open flames, the field was filling with a haze. It had caught somebody's attention.

"Where's Carter's lighter?" he asked them, scanning the grass frantically.

The engine noise came again to him, drifting on the wind, louder.

Then he saw it: a military-type truck was approaching in the distance. It was turning back and forth down the hair-pinned road on the nearby hillside, coming toward them.

"Guys!" Alex kicked at their feet as they lay in the grass. "Get up! Get up! Somebody's coming. You had your fun now—for two hours! Now we better get out of here."

"Calm down," Ruger chuckled, waving him to sit. "You've been uptight ever since we busted outta jail. You need to relax or you're gonna have a heart attack, man. Just *try* some of this stuff, Parris-dude, and you won't feel a thing. It's pretty great shit."

Alex quickly pulled on his socks and boots, laced them up. He took Ruger by the arm and tried to hoist him to his feet. Ruger protested and Benson laughed louder, full belly laughs that shook the ground beneath them.

No—it was another vehicle, a bigger truck, pulling into the field around the treeline behind them. The police markings on the doors kicked Alex into high gear.

"Ruger! Benson!" he called. "It's the police!"

They looked up at him, turned to see the police truck pulling into the field, but their legs were too soft to run and they stumbled back to the grass.

"Time to run away!" he warned them. "I'm going! You guys coming?"

"No...body's...coming," Benson could barely speak.

"I'm leaving! Right *now*!"

"Go ahead, college boy," Ruger muttered.

"You idiots! You dumb Lotos-Eaters!" Alex shouted.

Fate was reaching for him once more, grasping after his reality. Like Odysseus, Alex would be forced to set sail on his own, trying to reach home. He threw a fistful of dirt at them, trying to startle them away from their stupor.

"Get up," he shouted at them, then kept his promise and turned to run across the furrowed soil toward the hedgerows that bordered the field. It was no use, he saw before he rolled over the hedges and found himself tumbling down the hidden slope and into thorn bushes growing at the bottom.

The pungent puffs of smoke had knocked out his companions, leaving them unable to defend themselves or escape when the police finally caught up.

Alex dug his way out of the thorn bushes, his arms becoming scratched, thorns catching his back pocket and ripping it loose. He scrambled to the opposite side of the bushes, hiding behind the bushes for a few minutes. He waited long enough to watch the police officers descend on the field from two sides. Others attended to the smoking plants, swinging scythes at the stalks and allowing the pile of plant material to burn itself to ashes.

Letting his breathing return to normal, Alex crept away down the ravine, down to where a few burros were grazing. He thought one of the police officers might have spotted him so he crouched beside the nearest burro, using the animal as camouflage. The man on the hilltop pointed in his direction, calling back to the other police officers. Beneath the chewing jiggle of the burro's jaw, Alex saw the police officer break through the bushes and start down the slope, stopping short of the thorn bushes. Alex panicked.

The police officer stared hard in each direction. Scanning the field, he soon seemed satisfied that no one else had fled the scene.

Alex slowly exhaled. Then he escaped, using a trick he had learned from an old movie. He grabbed hold of the mane and tail of the burro, locking his legs around the burro's belly, and let the musty animal trot casually away, unnoticed and unsuspected, as he hung precariously on its hidden side. Meanwhile, he could imagine his short-lived friends rooting at the ground on all fours, grunting like wild pigs, much to the amusement of the police officers.

When he believed he was far enough from the hashish field, Alex dismounted. Spots of blood stained his arms and he felt thorns poking his hip, too. He reached back and discovered two thorns sticking through his pants. He removed them and noticed his pocket had been ripped half off. And his passport was gone. Shaking his head, he just hoped the police would not find it. He considered going back for it, looking through the thorn bushes. He might be caught if he did that. He used the f-word several times as he paced in a tight circle, shaking his fists in the air.

"This is what your stupid fate is? This? This stupid, fucking adventure?" he cursed himself. He stood up straight and inhaled as deeply as he could, exhaled as slowly as he could. "Okay, just get back to Eléna, just get back," he grumbled. "Then we can figure out what to do." He could probably get a new one at the embassy in Istanbul, he decided.

The burro had taken him to the edge of a farm and he crouched down behind an old fallen plow, hiding from anyone in the farm buildings. Checking the farm for activity, he chose to run. He leaped up and jogged down the dirt road past the farm, across a small fallow field, and crawled through a creek's deep ravine to where an arched stone bridge hid him from the afternoon sun. He splashed some of the stream's water over himself, sipped some from his cupped hand, and rested, his legs aching and his body exhausted. He sucked at two thorn wounds that continued to bleed, then applied pressure with his hand.

As the afternoon waned, he licked up the last of the melted chocolate bar Ruger had stolen off the constable's desk. He crumpled the wrapper and stuck it in his pants pocket. He would throw it away when he found a trash bin.

Eventually, the creaking of wagon wheels and the clopping of a horse roused him from his nap.

As the wagon passed slowly over the bridge, Alex scrambled up the embankment and climbed onto the back of the wagon, burying himself in the pile of hay, which filled the space between the side slats and rose up high behind the driver's back. Alex did not know where he was going but he was relieved to be going *somewhere*. The plodding of the horse's hooves and the rocking of the wagon lulled him to sleep as he hid under the hay.

The next thing Alex knew, he awoke in the lamplight of a barn and four young women stood over him, chattering among themselves.

CHAPTER 17

"And I must've fallen asleep in the hay," Alex continued from his hospital bed, using the gravelly monotone he had settled into. He floated somewhere between solemn alertness and frivolous lightheadedness as the drugs took effect. "I don't even remember falling out of the wagon or even stumbling into the barn. All I remember was waking up early the next morning when these girls found me. I guess they were daughters of the farmer who owned the barn I was hiding in. Turkish farmer's daughters. One of them was getting some of the hay and thrust her pitchfork into the pile where I was sleeping. Got me just above the knee, tore my pants."

He reached down to point out the spot.

"How're you feeling, Alex?" the nurse asked, brushing his sweaty forehead with a towel.

"I'm feeling real good," he replied. His speech was slurred. "You got good drugs here."

"You're feeling awfully hot, though."

"It is kind of hot in here. Is the air conditioning on?"

"Of course," she answered. "As low as we can set it. You

keep asking us to lower it."

"*Çok sıcak*!" Alex said suddenly. The only Turkish phrase he remembered.

"'Choke sea cock'? What's that?" the nurse asked.

"It's too hot!" he exclaimed, twisting in his bed.

"Calm down, Alex. You're only making things worse."

"*Çok sıcak*!" he repeated, falling into delirium.

"What are you saying?" she asked, but he was silent, breathing heavily as though he had just run several miles. She touched her hand to his forehead, then grabbed the digital thermometer off the nightstand and pushed it in his mouth, waited for it to beep. "Let me call Doctor Johnson. You're running a fever and we can't have that going into surgery."

"Surgery?" Alex mumbled. "What the heck are you talking about?"

"You don't remember?"

"I only remember waking up. In the pile of hay. In that barn. With the four girls taking care of me...."

He heard the intercom paging Dr. Johnson, and he waited in the darkness beneath his bandages. He called out to the nurse but there was no answer this time. The room was already spinning around, and he was slowly sinking, drowning.

All night he had dreamed of Eléna, the first woman he had ever truly loved, he said to whichever nurse had watched him overnight. He convinced himself of that, counting past loves great and small from sixth grade to the present. Meeting Eléna was like some gift presented to him for all his diligence and effort over so many years of his education. His parents had given him a new car last Christmas—which his roommate had totaled after borrowing it for a fatal spring break trip. What he had really wanted was a woman like Eléna: full-bodied, robust, luscious and ripe. He did not want the young teenage girls who found him in the barn the next morning as they went to milk the cow and the goats.

"*Efendim*?" a surprised woman's voice asked him.

"What?" Alex responded, his head swimming. "Where am I?"

He felt a wet towel wash his face then come to rest on his forehead.

"*Kendini kaybetti*," said the woman.

He guessed she was speaking to someone else, not him.

As Alex had gained consciousness in that barn, he had lifted his hand to his face and pulled the wet towel away. In the creeping morning light, he saw his caretakers: four girls, all dressed in what he thought were folk costumes—perhaps their normal everyday clothing, he decided. Their red or brown skirts and white aprons made him feel like he was in some long-forgotten time and place. Their heads were wrapped with scarves, dark hair gathered in ponytails hanging down their backs.

He regarded each of them in turn. When they saw his eyes on them, they covered their mouths with their hands or held up aprons. The eldest one seemed about sixteen, could have been older, and her three sisters looked two years or so apart: fourteen, twelve, and ten.

"I'm lost," he said, thinking it would serve to answer most of the questions these girls were asking each other about him.

"*İsminiz ne? Nerelisiniz?*" the eldest girl asked, and when he said nothing, she tapped his shoulder as if to let him know she was speaking to him.

"I don't know what you're saying," he muttered.

"*Çok güzel,*" a younger voice spoke, close to his ear.

"Do you speak English? English? Any English?" Alex asked, fearing that if he did not manage to communicate soon, she would advance from gentle tapping to something much harder. Perhaps from their father or a few older brothers.

"Doo, joo, shpeeka, ingleezha," the youngest girl repeated, followed a breath later with: "Ah! *İngilizce biliyor musunuz? İngilizce*!"

The girls giggled at her translation and Alex realized he was alive, kicked back into reality and forced to deal with it again.

"No," she said, a tiny bird-like chirp.

They giggled again.

Alex tried sitting up but felt the pain in his thigh and bent forward to check it.

"*Affedersiniz,*" the second-oldest spoke, a pout on her face. When Alex did not seem to understand, she pointed to the wound where her pitchfork had cut him. It was not deep, he saw, but it hurt. There was some blood, too.

"That's okay, I'll be all right," he assured her, catching on quickly.

He straightened up in his sitting position and placed his hand to his heart.

"I'm Alex." He swept his hand out to the side. "I'm from

America." He pretended to hold a camera to his face. "I'm a tourist." He clicked the imaginary camera a few times and shrugged his shoulders. "Now, I'm lost."

He looked at the eldest sister for support, believing she would be the one most likely to understand him. Instead, it was the youngest sister, who perhaps had English lessons in her school, who played translator. Alex was not convinced she knew what she was translating.

The eldest sister asked him, "*Nereye gidiyorsunuz*?" and through the youngest girl came the translation: "Go—for to where?"

At last there was some kind of communication, Alex sighed. He pointed outside the barn and told them his story, about his visit to the site of Ilium and how he got lost. He left out the part about the fight and the jail. They were listening, watching him intently, not understanding a word he was saying but fascinated by him, as though he were a movie star. They enjoyed his voice, and his animated gestures, which made them giggle. This stranger was an unexpected diversion from their morning chores.

"Do you understand? Can you help me get back to Ilium?" Alex asked when he had finished his story.

When they didn't appear to understand, Alex drew a map in the dirt with his finger, marking the coastline as he remembered it from the map. He drew a star where Ilium lay, and made gestures of misdirection, pointing to several possible locations away from the star.

"Ah!" the youngest girl exclaimed. "*Burada ne?* Here Büyükkestanelik!"

"Bookoo-what?" Alex asked.

After further explanation and digging in the dirt, he knew what village he was in—or near to—and roughly where it was on the coast of Turkey.

"*Bir şey yemek ister misiniz*?" asked the eldest girl, and the youngest girl translated: "Want you...mmm...you want...eat?"

Alex nodded excitedly, repeating the part of his story about eating only olives and a chocolate bar.

The two middle sisters jumped up and hurried out of the barn.

For a moment, he was afraid they would bring back the police, or their parents, or their brothers—anybody who would not wish for this dirty foreign boy to be in this barn with these four pretty girls, playing doctor with him. Preparing to flee, Alex struggled to get to his feet, holding his thigh, summoning his strength. The two sisters who remained were concerned for his injury, and the eldest one poked at the torn flaps of his pants over his thigh. She instructed him to do something. However, the youngest girl could not translate fast enough, so the eldest girl relied on frantic gesturing. She wanted him to pull off his pants so she could bandage his wound.

"I can't do that," he said, shaking his head. "I know this is Turkey. We can't see each other."

She insisted, squatting and reaching for his pant cuffs, pulling at his ankles.

"All right," he said. "If you insist."

His attention was drawn to noise outside. Just a cow. Or a goat.

Alex hesitantly unbuckled his belt and unsnapped his

pants and the girl jerked them down to his ankles. The youngest girl gasped and Alex was startled. The blood had run down his leg to his ankle, where it had matted his sock. His shirttails, he was glad to notice, reached low enough to cover his underpants. Before he could feel self-conscious about his exposure, the other sisters returned with a tray of food and a prepackaged first aid kit.

Over the next two hours, Alex was in the lap of luxury as he was fed the bread and yogurt, tomatoes and olives, cheese and eggs they brought for him. He was also served hot tea and cold creamy butter. The youngest pointed to each item and carefully spoke its name, teaching him. Alex repeated after her, out of politeness: *ekmek, cacık, zeytin, kaşarpeyniri*. She repeated the lesson with every bite Alex took and he mumbled after her.

As he ate, one sister disinfected his thigh and another sister wrapped it in sterile gauze. His shirt was coaxed off him and, along with his bloodstained pants, washed and hung up to dry in an open barn window where the sunshine beat through. The eldest sister gave him a blanket to cover himself.

The four girls sat in a semi-circle around him, content to listen to his rambling stories. Alex, of course, avoided any mention of losing his two comrades to a police raid in a hashish field. The bad part was over now, anyway. Soon he would be on the road again, thanks to their help. He would be heading back to Eléna. Realizing they did not care what he was actually saying, he began talking about Eléna. They became more interested when he began describing their first night together, using gestures and facial expressions to act out the events. Only the eldest sister seemed to understand that he was describing sex. When the 'buttons popped,' the girls burst out laughing at his gestures.

Suddenly, the eldest sister rose up on her knees, holding her skirt hem in her two hands, holding it so as to show a thin portion of her legs. She commanded the others to go away—and bring back water and soap, Alex soon saw.

They asked for the blanket and the three older girls splashed water on his face and chest. The eldest rubbed soap onto her hands and then onto Alex. Her hands rubbed the soapy water over his chest and down into his armpits, one then the other. She toweled off his chest and gestured for him to turn over. He smiled to her, embarrassed but genuinely thankful to be washed and refreshed once more. He turned in his kneeling position and bent over so she could continue washing him, her hands gradually taking on the actions of a masseuse that had his back well lathered and well kneaded. Cool water was poured over him and he squirmed at the chill. If that were the worst they could do, he thought, turning to face them and sitting back on the hay, he would be safe enough.

But it was not, he saw. As he gazed up at them, he saw the eldest sister holding the hem of her skirt again. She inched the hem higher, watching his face for a reaction. He could not see anything due to the shadows beneath her skirt and the black stockings she wore. He could only see a narrow strip of bare brown thighs between the top of her stockings and the raised hem of her skirt.

Before he could ponder what her intentions might be,

she dropped onto him, plopping down upon his lap, facing him, almost nose to nose. She sat right over his crotch, and her weight, light as it was, pressed down on him. She wriggled in her seat a moment, then leaned forward over him until her lips were inches from his. She ignored his distraught expression—the foreign boy clearly did not know what to do. Her fingers reached beneath herself and pulled at his briefs, wet from the washing.

Alex scrambled out from under her, practically tossing her sideways into the hay pile. He stood up, winced at the pain in his thigh wound. Shaking the hay and dust off himself, brushing harder where it had stuck to his moist skin, he stood before her. His hands fell in front of his crotch.

"Sorry, Miss, but I—I can't do that."

She looked at him sadly, guessing his meaning.

"You're pretty," he said, seeing her frown, "but I'm not that kind of guy."

He thought for a moment. He'd always wanted to be that kind of guy, like his fraternity brothers, the ones who took whatever they wanted. Those guys would never hesitate taking a girl to bed. But he, dammit, was raised to respect women.

"I'm sorry, really I am."

He wanted to pat her shoulder or even give her a friendly, brotherly hug to soften the rejection, but he didn't think she would allow that or accept it.

"You've been very kind." He glanced around at the sisters. "You all have."

The eldest girl turned and held her hands to her face.

Was she crying?

"I'm sorry, Miss." He considered whether she would turn him in now that he'd rejected her. He had to explain more. "If this were another time and place, then, sure, we could get to know each other. We might even be good friends, perhaps grow to be lovers. I've got nothing against Turkish girls but...."

The younger sisters glared at him, their eyes accusing him of hurting their sister. The eldest sister spoke angry words at him.

Alex held his hands up, as though holding back their hatred of him.

"I have to be going now, anyway—to somewhere—right now," he stammered, stepping gingerly across the barn floor in his stocking feet, over to where his shirt and pants were hanging up to dry.

The eldest girl suddenly turned and chased after him, caught him from behind and wrapped her arms around him. She held him tightly, squeezing the breath from him as he took down his clothes. He shook her off, as gently as he could, and tried to step into his pants, hopping first on one foot then the other as the girl continued to hug him. She maneuvered around him until she was face to face. He stood in his pants, bare-chested, as she took his face in her hands and clumsily pressed her thin, brown lips to his mouth.

Alex was surprised and grabbed her hands. He pulled her hands away from his face, then held her hands firmly away.

"I'm really sorry," he said in as soft a tone as he could

muster. But his voice was also shaking. "I have a girlfriend already: Eléna."

He inscribed curves in the air with his hands, tapped his chest, and jabbed his thumb back toward Ilium. She had to understand that his girlfriend was back there. She was waiting desperately for him.

"Eléna is my woman. I've been talking about her all day. But, of course, I know you don't understand any of my words."

He looked into the girl's dark eyes, wet with tears, and a realization came to him.

"Oh, I get it! You thought I was saying I wanted to, umm, fool around with *you*? Is that it? But I—I didn't mean anything. I was not, uh, trying to seduce you. I was just telling you a *story*. You know 'story'? It's pretend. Not real. Not true. But I—I do think you're cute, Miss... uh, Miss Turkey."

He stepped back carefully, wary of farm tools and animal feces. He offered his most sincere smile, showing his bright white teeth now sticky with his breakfast.

"Derya," said the youngest sister, pointing at the eldest girl. "She Derya."

Alex got the meaning. The eldest sister's name was Derya.

"I'm sorry, Derya," he spoke softly. "But you'll meet the right guy some day. I know you will. Just like I met the right woman on my trip to Istanbul."

She lowered her head, standing demurely before him, and he became choked up at her shy posture.

"*İstanbul*?" asked one of the middle sisters.

They all pointed to the north.

"That way?" he asked and they nodded.

Alex knew he had to go, had to return to his beloved Eléna. The longer he was away from her, the more trouble he would get into—the same as Odysseus, he pondered, who had languished under the spell of Circe for several years; in fact, until she had borne him three sons, according to Homer. How long had it been for Alex? Two, three days by now? Eléna would surely have returned to Istanbul, he calculated. The tour would have ended and she would be cruising back through the Dardanelles and across the Aegean Sea to Athens. And then where? Her home? They had exchanged addresses in Istanbul, writing them on hotel stationary, but he did not know where his piece of paper was now. He could recall only part of it from memory and he felt guilty for that. Chicago, Illinois was all he remembered.

Derya, perhaps giving up on Alex, sternly ordered her sisters to start their chores.

As they worked, Alex, afraid to go out in the light of day, entertained them with a very detailed explanation of computer network systems, interrupted with a few brief interludes about his wonderful software design job at CyberAmerica waiting for him when he returned home. He still had a month, he assured them. Plenty of time to find his way back to civilization and Eléna, then catch his flight home. Since he'd met Eléna and spent so much, he would have to skip the final leg to Egypt.

The girls seemed to agree with his plans.

"*Çok sıcak*!" Alex said, wiping his brow, much to his

teachers' amusement. It was the first Turkish phrase he had learned: "Phew! It sure is hot!"

"*Çok sıcak*!" the girls giggled.

Later, when it was dusk, he was ready to leave. The younger three sisters presented him with a small knapsack filled with food and a bottle of tea. One of the middle sisters held up a small knife, acting out a cutting motion, then dropped it into the knapsack. He might need it, she seemed to be saying, to cut the sausages.

"Thanks for all of your help," he said cheerfully. "I won't forget you—"

"We're just doing our job," came a man's voice.

"What job?" asked Alex.

"Taking care of you."

"Who are you?"

"I'm your doctor, Alex. Don't you recognize my voice? Doctor Johnson. I know we haven't actually seen each other yet, but we will. Soon enough."

"I'm—in a hospital?" Alex was confused, thinking he was definitely back in the barn.

"That's right, Alex."

"His fever's been as high as a hundred and four," a woman's voice spoke. "We've been trying to keep his temperature down but it rises again after some time."

"Perhaps we should postpone it a day or two," the doctor said in a lowered voice, "but then we run the risk of more damage. Let me speak with Doctor Lindsay. Page him, please."

There was some rustling in the room, then silence. Alex breathed deeply, not believing he had been revisiting his harem back in Turkey. No, he caught himself, he was *still* in Turkey. In a hospital on a Navy base. In Izmir, the birthplace of Homer, who wrote the story of Ilium. That was where he and Eléna had visited, where Helen and Paris were separated eternally.

"Alex, can you hear me?" It was Dr. Johnson's voice again. "We've decided to go ahead with the surgery. Your fever and the pain behind your eyes are related to your infection. We don't want to wait any longer on it."

He was quickly prepped for surgery and wheeled into the operating theater. Alex sensed the brightness of the room through his bandages. The soft murmur of voices and the general bustle of fabrics and metal instruments merged in his sagging consciousness to become a macabre orchestra. He cried out for someone named Eléna and heard Dr. Johnson give an explanation to the O.R. nurses: "A girl he knew back home, I think."

"Okay, Alex," a nurse's sugary voice spoke, falling abruptly upon him like the fortuitous words of his divine protector, the goddess Aphrodite: "We're going to begin the anesthesia now. You're going to have a chance to catch up on your sleep, maybe have some pleasant dreams for a change. Or—maybe you shouldn't think of anything. That might be better. Empty your mind, Alex. Okay? Are you ready? Good boy. Now, breathe deeply and count back from one hundred...slowly...."

CHAPTER 18

The eldest girl, Derya, had led him out of the barn in the twilight and around the side of the house to where her three sisters nervously shuffled about. They checked that he had the knapsack. The youngest girl offered him two figs and he put them in the knapsack. The journey would continue. He was going home, and he showed his pleasure with a wide, open grin, the kind his father had worked so hard to perfect.

"*İyi yoculuklar*!" the girls said, waving farewell.

"*İyi şanslar*, Aleki," Derya whispered in his ear. She pressed her lips to his scruffy cheek, barely brushing his whiskers.

"Is good luck," the youngest girl translated.

"Thanks," said Alex, "but I hope I don't need it."

He waved to them as he walked off down the dirt road, pausing twice to turn and wave again, until he was lost in the darkness.

The road was easy to follow, the moonlight showing him the way. Alex was feeling relaxed and refreshed, and on the verge of whistling a happy tune. The cut in his thigh did not bother him too much, bandaged as it was. His stomach was full enough. His head was clear, his mind sharp as he calculated the direction and the distance to his destiny.

And yet, every few yards, some random noise or the swaying of the tree branches overhead reminded him that he was on the run. He was walking, sure, and at a quick pace, but he was actually running away. In fact, he was running from something and running toward something at the same time.

If he could simply skirt the main roads, avoid anyone suspicious of foreigners, he might be able to be back at Ilium in perhaps a day and a half. What he would do then, he had no idea. He needed to get to Çanakkale, actually. Then he would have to find a way to Istanbul, to the hotel where his suitcase waited. He hoped they would hold it for him. For both him and Eléna.

"I'm coming, Eléna," he sang, then remembered when he had uttered the same words in their hotel bed in Istanbul. Even alone on the road, he blushed. He was on his way back to her. He breathed deeply the warm, dry air as he walked.

Perhaps she was already hard at work finding where her lover had ended up, alerting the authorities to his disappearance. She saw him rush to save her, right? He wasn't sure. He tried to conjure the scene. Hadn't she seen him fighting the three Turks? Or had she slipped past the wall and out of sight by then, heading to the tour bus? He could not be certain now. Everything that had happened since then clouded his memory of those few brief images.

Okay, he thought, she would get on the bus and the bus would take them back to the hotel in Çanakkale. She would stay the night there; during that time, she would worry about him, feel bad that she left him there. She would make a few phone calls—local authorities, the tourism office, the bus company—and she would get answers. Then she could take another bus back to retrieve him. Or, if she were still angry with him for…for what? For being himself? For showing that he was no dummy, that he had a future, that he could support her with his new job at CyberAmerica in California?

No, he decided, she was the sort of person likely to carry a grudge. She would probably stay angry, take the bus all the way to Istanbul. By the time she arrived, perhaps she would be over her anger. Then she would worry about him and start the process of finding him. Or she would be over him. She might toss his suitcase in a dumpster and check out.

He noticed his pace had quickened, but he was not prepared to run. If only he had a car or even a motorcycle, he could be at Ilium by dawn. Then he could catch a tourist bus back to Çanakkale. He still had his ticket stub in the pocket of his pants.

Alex gazed ahead, straining to see in the dark as clouds obscured the moonlight. The dirt road curved through the woods, apparently leading him nowhere. The promise of an intersection with a paved road was all that kept him going. Derya had indicated he should follow it to get home. But exactly where the road would take him, he did not know. He hoped it would lead to a paved road, a highway, which would take him to a town, which would enable him to catch a bus or hitchhike to Ilium.

The trees ended and ahead were open fields, now lit by a golden moon.

He stopped and took a drink of the tea the girls had given him. Studying the situation, he concluded that he really was not too far away from the hashish field. That field was not far from the town with the jail, either. They had walked all day, and at about three miles per hour, he calculated, he and his military buddies had likely crossed only about 25 miles. They had wanted to go south while he had insisted on going north. He recalled the map the girls drew in the dirt, indicating where they were and where the coast was. He stared up at the stars, found a constellation he recognized. He thought he was heading in the right direction but he could not know for certain until sunrise. Yet he feared traveling in the daylight.

He squinted as he gazed across the fields. Ahead, the road forked sharply to the left and disappeared over a hill. Beyond were more trees. The road to the right seemed to be the way ahead, although it also crossed open fields and then was lost over a hill. He scanned the sky, measuring the constellations and determining the direction north. He set off with renewed confidence. Over the hill, however, he found the road curling through a farm and then a village beyond. That was not the best path to go, he considered. A dog barked at the farm below him and he crouched out of sight, waiting more than twenty minutes for the dog to be quiet.

Keeping low, Alex crept back to the crest of the hill, and

decided to take the other road. He returned to the fork and paused, checking the constellations again. He would give the other road a try, at least see where it went, even though he felt it was not the right way.

Halfway across the field, following the road, Alex felt a strange sensation scratching at his consciousness, the poke of something hidden yet familiar. He looked around, almost feeling that someone was watching him from the treeline behind him and the one ahead. The breeze picked up, brought him the scents of flowers, then of goats.

Alex cocked his head, thinking, deciding, then started ahead.

He stopped and looked back.

Something was in the brush at the treeline behind him. There was movement in the brush. He thought it might be a wild animal, or another dog following him from one of the nearby farms.

Then he heard a voice: "Shut up!"

"Who's there?" Alex called.

The rustling in the brush stopped and he heard only the breeze dancing through the grasses. He started toward the motion, more curious than fearful.

However, the silence could not be maintained and the quivering bushes continued, along with grunts and angry snorts.

Alex ran up to the place where the commotion was. There he saw two bodies, fighting each other—wrestling! The shirtless man was on top of a woman wearing a skirt. His first thought was that he should leave them alone, especially with them being Turks. If he disturbed the man's lovemaking, the man might come at him and try to kill him, or at least bring notice that the foreigner they're all looking for is here.

But his next thought was whether the man really ought to be fumbling around with any woman in the bushes, next to the field, beside a road, in the middle of the night. That did not seem right. So he stood his ground and spoke:

"Excuse me, is everything all right here?"

The movement halted and the back of the man rose toward him, twisting until Alex could see the man's face.

"Benson?" He stared at the young man. "Is that you?"

Whoever it was, the man's anger showed on his face: dirty and bruised, streams of blood dried on his skin, and a jagged cut stretching across his forehead. He did not seem to recognize Alex.

"What are you doing here?" Alex asked, keeping his voice low but firm.

Under the man's body was another, and Alex saw bare flesh among torn clothing. The young woman grabbed at her white blouse and pulled it across her breasts.

Alex reached for Benson's shoulder to pull him away, but he swept the hand back and turned his attention to the girl, who was growling words of desperation.

"Stop it, Benson!" Alex shouted, trying to keep his voice low. He saw that the man he thought was Benson wore only a blue towel wrapped around his hips. In his struggle with the girl, it had come loose. "Get off her! You know that's not right!"

Suddenly Benson lunged up at Alex, knocking him down, and punched him in the face. Another blow landed in his stomach. The girl sprang up but Benson leaped at her, brought her down hard on the ground. He tore at her skirt, crawled over her like an animal, and pushed the skirt up to her hips, grabbing furiously at her undergarments.

"Hey, man!" Alex grunted. "That's not cool! Stop it!"

Alex got to his knees and grabbed Benson's leg. He kicked at Alex as he tried to hold the girl in place. Alex released the leg and launched himself over Benson's body, adding his weight to Benson's, both of them on top of the girl. Alex wrapped his arms around Benson's waist and rolled both of them off the girl, holding him so that Benson was now on top of him. They wrestled and Benson got in another punch to Alex's jaw.

The girl stood up, watching the fight instead of running.

"Go on, get away," Alex called to her, holding Benson in a bear hug.

He saw the red skirt and white apron, remembering the girls who had found him in the barn. He thought he was farther away by now, but she looked familiar as she straightened her blouse, noted a missing button, and lowered the torn skirt.

The moonlight broke through the drifting clouds then and Alex had a clear view of her face. It was Derya from the farm. He became enraged that Benson would try to rape her—or any girl.

"You bastard!" Alex shouted, pushing Benson away. "What the heck do you think you're doing?" He freed his arm and swung a fist into Benson's jaw, and again, and a third time.

Benson popped up, naked and dirty, bloodied, and Alex

was shocked at his appearance. The Navy man had become a wild animal! He stood in a defensive stance, hands raised to attack despite being naked. Their eyes met but it was clear to Alex that Benson was no longer acting rationally.

"What happened to you?" asked Alex. "You look like shit. And where are your clothes?"

Benson was breathing roughly, as if his ribs hurt too much to take deeper breaths.

"You got away from the hashish field, looks like," said Alex. "That's good. What about Ruger? Did he get away?"

Benson's breathing was raspy but he grumbled a few words: "You—left us."

Alex relaxed, feeling guilty—as usual. "I'm sorry."

Benson did not relax.

"You know I was trying to get you guys to escape with me," said Alex. "You were too stoned to move. I kept shouting at you two."

Benson still did not relax. Alex wanted to glance at Derya, to see if she were all right, or if she were even there still, but he dared not take his eyes off Benson.

"Derya, are you okay?" he called to the side, keeping his eyes on Benson.

She replied something in Turkish, an angry tone.

"I understand," he responded. "I know you want to slap him, right? He deserves it. But I know this guy—sort of—and he wasn't that kind of guy before. I'm trying to see what happened to make him this way."

Then his eyes went instinctively over to the girl—

Benson rushed him in that instant, bowling him over, knocking him to the ground. His fists pummeled Alex's gut.

Derya leaped on Benson, digging her fingers into his eyes until he fell off Alex.

"Stop it, Benson! I'm not your enemy!"

Alex pushed Benson down in the grass. Benson scrambled away. Alex ran and leaped onto him and they wrestled until Alex was able to get on top of him. He held onto his arms, but Benson still did not relax.

"You don't know nothing," Benson grunted.

"What are you talking about?"

"You are so stupid!"

"At least I still got my clothes," said Alex.

They remained in that position for a minute.

"Okay, I'm going to let you up," said Alex. "But you're not going to attack me again. I'm not your enemy. And you're not going to hurt that girl. I know her. She and her sisters helped me yesterday. I guess she was following me and you just decided to try and rape her. This isn't a game, Benson! You're wearing only a towel and you decide raping some farm girl is the most important thing you have to do tonight? What's gotten into you?"

"*They*—got—into me."

"What are you talking about?"

"Police."

"At the field?"

Benson nodded quickly.

"What'd they do?" asked Alex.

"They—raped—*me*."

The clouds closed around the moon, like curtains at the end of a stage play, and he could not see Benson's face. Yet Alex had seen the truth in Benson's eyes as he said the words. Alex understood: he was scared—and vengeful. Benson had been turned into a madman and was now backed into a corner, lost and alone. Now he wanted to destroy something, anything—anyone.

Alex slowly climbed off Benson, feeling somehow tainted by rubbing against his abused body. He did not know what to say. 'Sorry' did not seem sincere enough and anything more took him down a dark alley he never knew existed. All he knew was that it was something his fraternity brothers joked about too frequently. He knew one guy who was teased a lot—until he quit the fraternity.

"You just decide to rape some poor girl, like for revenge?" asked Alex, taking a moment to see which way his moral compass was spinning. "That's crazy. It's not the same. It's not compensation." He thought for a minute. "I guess if it's a revenge thing, then you should do it to the same guys who did it to you, not to some innocent third-party. I mean, that's just...."

Of course, he knew Benson could not exactly go to the authorities to complain. He was a fugitive. He was one of the attackers in the fight at Ilium. Now he was a victim. Who would listen to his story?

"I'm sorry that happened to you."

Alex turned and regarded the girl. She squatted with her arms curled around her knees, waiting to see that the wild man was properly punished. Alex waved toward the farm.

"Maybe you should just go on home, Derya."

He gestured again, directing her down the road back to her farm. She shook her head, spoke more angry words.

She seemed angry that he was treating her disgusting attacker with apparent kindness.

"Were you following me, Derya?" he asked.

Alex went to her, sat beside her and placed his arm around her shoulders.

"You're safe now, but you shouldn't go out at night. There may be wild animals, or guard dogs, or strange men from other countries running around in the night all naked and such." He turned to Benson: "You know better than to do what you were trying to do. That's criminal. Besides, I know this girl. Her name's Derya. She and her sisters helped me. They gave me some food and tea, too."

He reached for the knapsack, dug out the tea bottle. Derya watched him twist open the bottle, then hand it to the man who had attacked her. She rattled off some angry words, then kicked the bottle out of his hand.

"Derya, I know you're angry," said Alex. "And I know you were attacked by this stupid jerk, but I know him. Please relax. Or, better yet, why not return to your home? No, that's not good. If you'll wait a few minutes, I'll escort you back to the farm. That way you'll be safe."

Instead of a verbal response, Derya crossed her arms over her chest, angry eyes stabbing at Benson.

Alex handed the knapsack to Derya, gesturing for her to eat something. She shook her head, then spoke more angry words as she pointed at Benson.

"I know, I know," said Alex. "He's a stupid jerk. We both know that."

Benson rolled onto his side, facing away from them. Alex saw the lines going down his back, lines made by a whip, perhaps. Or running through thorn bushes. Even in the dim moonlight, he could see bruises.

"Send her away," Benson grunted after a while.

She jumped up and kicked his butt, using more Turkish profanity.

"That don't hurt no more." Benson rolled onto his back, keeping a hand over his groin. "Nothing hurts now."

"Say you're sorry," said Alex. "She's a good girl. She doesn't deserve to be attacked."

He slapped Benson's shoulder, then looked at Derya to catch her reaction. By her expression, he knew he had not slapped the man hard enough. Alex swung his hand again, leaving a loud *swack* echoing across the field. Derya nodded, then kicked him again, striking his thigh.

"I'm sorry!" Benson cried out.

"First things first," said Alex. "How'd you get away from the police? They had you surrounded and you two were higher than a kite."

"We ran," said Benson with a huff.

Although they reacted slowly, they had run as fast as they could. But they had come to a stave fence at the end of the field and while Ruger managed to leap over it, more or less successfully, falling on the other side, Benson had gotten his pant leg caught in the staves and the police easily apprehended him while Ruger continued running. The police, or whatever government or military officials they were, hit Benson in the head with the butt of a rifle, knocking him out. They dragged him back to their truck, where he soon regained consciousness. Some big ugly brute was asking questions and he could not answer them.

The man kept slapping his face. When the man became too frustrated with Benson not understanding, he yanked him up from the bed of the truck and threw him on the ground. Two others kicked him as he rolled back and forth trying to avoid the boots. Finally, he could resist no longer, too exhausted and too much in pain, and when they pushed him over a bale of hay and tore off his pants he could not protest. After they finished with him and were laughing and smoking nearby, Benson made a dash for freedom. They did not see him run into the forest across the road; the truck blocked their view of his escape.

Alex sat sullenly, rubbing his forehead, feeling his heart beating fast.

"And Ruger?"

"I dunno."

"Did he get away?"

"I said I don't know!"

The breeze and a few crickets were all the sounds heard in the field.

"What they did wasn't right," Alex said after a while. "But what you were doing, that wasn't right, either. Two wrongs don't make a right."

"Fuck you," Benson growled.

The thought flashed through Alex's head that he had saved Eléna from that same kind of trouble. He had stopped the three men from hurting her. Who knew what they might have done to her? Now he had stopped this man from hurting another girl. That was who he was: Alex, protector of women. His mother would be proud of him. Yet that was not what he wanted. Why did he always have to save girls from the bad boys? He would always be thanked with a handshake or a few spoken words: "Thank you so much, Alex, you're such a sweet boy." No, that was not who he wanted to be. But his moral compass was so embedded into him that he could not act badly. Now here was someone, young Seaman Benson, who had been changed from a fairly decent man into a pig, or a wolf, or something grotesque. Alex wondered if he could change Benson back into a man.

"Well, we can't tell anyone, you know."

"I know," said Benson. He was still seething, his voice rough, hateful. "I need to get back at them, at Turks, any Turk. I want to beat up someone. I want to rape that girl over there. Or any girl. I don't care what she looks like. That's all I can do now. Get some payback."

"We need to get you to a hospital—"

"You kidding me?"

"You're wounded."

"Yeah," Benson groaned, "I'll be wounded forever."

Alex stood and looked for Derya. He motioned at her and she reluctantly handed him the knapsack.

"You need to eat something," he said, tossing it to Benson. "I'll bet you're hungry. Eat something. Then we'll figure out what to do."

Benson pulled one of the sausages from the knapsack, munched on it.

"We'll need to get you some clothes, first of all."

"I got the towel from a clothesline."

"Where is that towel now? You probably should put it on again with her here."

"She don't care. I don't care."

"Maybe she can get you something to wear," said Alex. "She could probably find something that would fit you. Their farm is about three miles away."

He went to her and gestured the need for a shirt and pants. He glanced back at his friend. The man also needed some footwear for the hike. Derya was not sympathetic, however. Alex tried to make her understand that Benson was not fundamentally a bad man. That was not an idea easy to get across in gestures.

"If we can get some clothes then we'll leave all of you alone," he said to her. "Please help us, Derya. I'm sorry for everything that happened—you don't know how sorry I am for these past three days—but there's no lasting damage, right? You can forget this ever happened."

He saw Derya's eyes suddenly widen and he spun around just in time to see Benson lunge a knife at him—actually at *her*. Alex swung her roughly aside and the knife blade deflected off his leather belt. Benson fell awkwardly to his knee but immediately sprang up, knife poised.

"No!"

"Let me kill her!" he cried out. "Then it'll be done."

"Stop it!"

"She's nobody, man. Nobody'll notice her gone. You hold her down for me, then you can take your turn. After me."

"Put the knife down. You're acting crazy."

Benson thrust the knife repeatedly at Alex, all the while glancing at the girl.

"Payback!"

Alex grabbed Benson's wrist, tried for the hand with the

knife, but the man's arm was already in motion and he could not hold it back. The knife swept into the folds of her skirt and she shrieked, falling to the ground. Alex shoved Benson backwards with both hands to his chest, causing him to lose his footing and stumble. Alex swung a fist at Benson's jaw—half-heartedly, intending only to startle Benson into stopping his threats but not wanting to hurt him. As Benson fell, Alex caught the upward sweep of the knife. The blade cut his forearm and continued harmlessly upward into the air.

"Run, Derya!" Alex cried out, thinking the skirt's many pleats would have stopped the blade.

He glanced at his forearm and saw blood.

Benson jabbed at Alex, feigned a deep thrust and broke away. He leaped at the girl as she turned to flee, tripping her. He crawled over her, raising the knife over her chest, grabbing her breast with the other hand.

"Don't!" shouted Alex.

He pounced on Benson, and they tumbled off the girl. They rolled over and over, fumbling for the knife between them. The wrestling took them to a slope and they slid down it, crashing against some rocks at the bottom. Alex felt for the knife, an innocent tool a farm girl had slipped into the knapsack. He found the handle, grabbed it.

"Let it go!" Alex growled. "This is not—the way—"

Benson grasped Alex's throat and he dropped the knife. He wanted to cry out how ridiculous Benson was being but he had no voice. His hand scrambled for the knife, found it again. Benson tightened his fingers on Alex's throat. They rolled over and the knife slipped down to Alex's hip. He struggled to free his hand, straining for the knife. He just wanted to get it away from Benson. The man was driven by rage and might do anything.

Instead, it was Alex who was filled with rage—moral outrage, in fact, a call to preserve civility. He felt the knife blade next to his belly, nicked his thumb on the metal but grabbed hold of it anyway, and in one continuous motion drew it up along his torso. Benson resisted, pushing Alex's hand downward. Alex summoned his strength and forced the knife upward—where it suddenly thrust into the skin under the ribs.

Benson gasped. Alex felt a lurch of the ribcage, a pause, then stillness. He held the knife steady, not sure what had happened.

Everything seemed to halt at once: the moonlight, the turn of the Earth, his own heartbeat, and time.

"Oh—my—God," Alex muttered, frozen against the body.

He rolled off Benson, not sure what to do. He got up on his knees and took a wrist in his hands, checking for a pulse. He put two fingers to the neck and felt for some sign of life. He leaned in to check for breathing. As he did what he thought was required, he was quivering, as though an arctic chill had blown through the field. He shook his head repeatedly, mumbling how it was all a dream, had to be a dream, a bad dream.

On his hands and knees, he crawled over to the slope, and sat leaning back against it. He inhaled deeply, feeling his chest tighten, as though he had almost drowned, and held the breath as long as he could. For that moment, he felt dizzy and did not know where he was, or why he was wherever he was. He let out the breath.

Suddenly he noticed the knife in his hand and jumped back as though it were a snake. He tried to shake it free but it stuck to his hand.

"No!" he cried, staring at the knife, his hand bloody.

He tossed the knife as hard as he could, aiming for California but his poor throw sent the knife straight up in the air. It dropped straight down and landed point first in Benson's chest. Alex grabbed the knife again and angrily launched it into the night. This time it fell silently in the grass far away.

Realizing there was no delete key, no rewind, no do-over, he allowed time to begin again.

"I was only trying to move the knife out of the way," he said, trying to catch his breath. "I just wanted to get it away from him—so he couldn't use it. I was trying to help. Really. I was helping him. Helping."

He looked up as a shadow grew to engulf him in the moonlight.

The girl appeared. She had hoisted a stone the size of her head up to her shoulder. Before Alex could say or do anything, she let it drop onto Benson's head. Alex threw himself to the side as the stone bounced off and rolled a little farther down the slope.

"He's already dead! You don't need to do that."

He tried to stand, but the girl stood away from him, would not help him up.

"I'm sorry, Derya," he said, almost whimpering. "It was an accident. I didn't mean to.... You know that, right?"

He regarded her, saw her hands were shaking, her face a mix of emotions.

"It was all an accident. It was self-defense, right?" He pointed at the body, then back at her. "He attacked you. I tried to save you. I did save you! Then we fought. He used the knife on me. I was trying to save you. I'm not a killer."

Alex checked the cut on his arm: minor. But proof enough if he needed it.

He glanced around the field, as though he were checking for more evidence. Looking up the slope toward the road, he noticed lights. There were faint lights bobbing in the darkness. He pointed and Derya turned to look.

"We were too loud. Now they're checking on what's happening."

The girl stood up, making herself obvious.

He went to her. "Derya, please don't say anything. Just run home. Forget you ever saw me. I'm nobody. And I never hurt you. I saved you. Go!"

She seemed to understand him and quickly took the hem of her skirt in her hands and ran up the slope.

Alex took the opposite path and hurried into the treeline, breaking into the next field, cutting through the stalks of barley. He heard the noise on the upper field growing, the lights dancing across the trees and clouds. He ducked down among the stalks and watched. Better to be quiet than to tear through the field and draw attention by his motion and noise. He waited.

At the crest of the slope, a man on a horse appeared in silhouette, scouting the lower field. A few others stood around them, flashlights darting here and there. The murmur grew as people discovered the battered body of a naked man and began deciding what to do.

CHAPTER 19

A persimmony needle of sunrise pricked his eyes as he lay among the crumpled stalks of barley, four fields removed from where he had fought Benson. He sat up, rubbing his eyes, wondering if it all had been a dream. He remembered the girl, pretty Derya, way too young for him yet infatuated with him, apparently following him down the road in the dark and being attacked by a lunatic named Benson. He saw the cut on his arm and he knew it had really happened. It was not just a bad dream.

How could he let that whole episode happen? He choked as the memory overwhelmed him. He had killed Benson.

"I'm not a killer," he mumbled. "I'm a protector."

He did what he had to do, he would say to anyone accusing him of murder. It was a fight he didn't want to engage in. It was a struggle forced upon him. People would have to understand that. He was just a kid, really, a college graduate who knew nothing about the world. He was a bookworm. He could never be expected to fight, much less to kill, some crazed would-be rapist. He acted to save the girl. He knew he would say nothing about it and he hoped there would be no reason to say anything.

"A dark secret stashed away in the dark of night," he spoke, then added: *a secret that will stay hidden in all the deep nights that follow*. Home was never further away than it was now. Wiping tears from his eyes, Alex cleared his throat and spit.

He had to make good time today, he knew, even in broad daylight, or he would never make his way to his destination, or to his destiny—with Eléna. Was she still waiting for him? He had to believe she was. By now, she would be desperate for news.

After refreshing himself at an old water trough and dodging fresh goat piles while crossing the pasture, he found a trail leading to another farm.

"Not again," he mumbled, seeing two girls tending to chickens.

From up on his hillside, he spied something useful. Leaning against the side of a shed was a small motorbike, what he would call a Moped. He'd ridden one once before, during the summer before his senior year of college. Just like riding a bike, but without the peddling. He wondered if it were in working order, and whether or not there might be any gasoline in the small tank.

"Only one way to find out," he whispered, rising from the bushes when the girls had disappeared.

He broke from the brush, half-sliding half-tripping down the hill, and stood scanning the clearing around the barn and the shed. A few chickens clucked at him as he went straight for the Moped. The remains of a yellow lightning bolt outlined in black gave the motorbike a distinctive appearance. Nevertheless, it was as fine a horse, he thought, as the great wooden horse of Troy. He pulled it away from the shed, gave it a quick visual inspection: dirty but otherwise nothing to indicate it would not work.

Alex hopped onto it and flicked the ignition switch. The engine groaned but started. He glanced around to see if anyone noticed. No one came. He turned the bike in the yard and rode off on the rickety machine, its once-white body rusted and its engine sputtering unreliably, down a new dirt road, heading to anywhere else, his favorite destination.

Not far down the road, however, he came upon a farm wagon. Probably, it was leaving a village that must be ahead, thought Alex. As he passed the wagon, the two men on it suddenly stood up and shouted at him, pointing desperately at him.

Did they recognize him? Alex wondered. He floored the Moped and achieving almost thirty miles per hour over the rough terrain strewn with loose stones. He had learned how to keep his balance over the first two miles. Either the men recognized the bike or they knew about Benson—

Alex sensed a shadow sweeping over him and looked back.

There was the younger man from the wagon. He had unbridled one of the horses and was now in hot pursuit, shouting "*Dur! Dur!*"

Guessing that *dur* meant something like *stop*, Alex tried to make the vehicle go faster but it was topped out already. He had to keep to the bumpy road but the horseman could leap over fences to cross fields while gaining on the Moped thief.

As Alex raced into the village, slowing only as much as needed to negotiate the turns, the horseman galloped after him. The man's frantic calls brought people out into the street, curious at the commotion. The horseman called to them to stop the thief, and they tried to block his way. As Alex rolled down the narrow lanes, their shouts of "*Dur!*" only made him more desperate.

"*Durdurun hırısz*!" the villagers yelled after him, and as each person he passed joined in the chorus, Alex panicked. He knew he was being chased now not by a lone horseman but by an entire village, the working men, the old people, the teenagers and children. They gathered like tributaries flowing into the raging river that spilled after him.

Suddenly he realized he was in real danger. It was no longer a race, it was a game of tag, or a rugby match and he was the guy with the ball. He was a foreigner, too, a criminal, a wildman, and no amount of verbal explanation would placate them.

Knocking over tables of crafts down one lane and a vegetable cart in another, Alex emerged into a plaza.

More people shouted at him: "*Dikkat! Dikkat!*"

They motioned furiously for him to watch where he was going. Yet Alex could only display his terror, frozen on his face. He was sorry for the senseless destruction, yes, but more worried about them not understanding his situation. He was innocent, no matter what anyone said.

The horseman crashed through the lanes after him,

knocking over just as many carts and stands, shouting his anger. Once in the open, he bellowed at the fat constable lounging outside his station reading a newspaper and smoking a pipe.

"*Mesele nedir*?" the portly constable called after him, obviously asking him what the commotion was all about. Alex was quickly learning Turkish by example.

He saw the constable glare quickly back at the newspaper headline, and frantically stumble out of his chair and fire up his old Ford Impala, parked in the alley nearby, to give chase.

Alex burst out of the village like a cannon ball shot from the merchant's lane, projecting its fastest trajectory toward the coast. He glanced back, hoping to see that none had followed him. Instead, a mob of villagers was running behind him with fists shaking and a few farm implements raised in anger.

What had he done to deserve this? For all they knew, he had only borrowed a Moped, an old rusty machine that was worth less than the gasoline inside its tank.

The engine sputtered and the Moped wobbled from side to side as Alex struggled to maintain his balance. All too soon, the Moped had run out of gas.

Seeing the constable's car and a few farm trucks breaking through the dividing mob and speeding toward him, Alex abandoned the Moped beside the road, leaping off it like he was being tossed off by a bucking bronco. He landed on his feet and ran without pause. The horseman and the constable's car led the charge.

Alex scrambled down into a ravine filled with mulberry

bushes.

As the posse of two halted at the edge of the ravine to look for him, they were joined by the villagers eager for an evening's entertainment. The lynching of a Moped thief could be the most exciting event of the year for them. *These people need more TV channels*, Alex thought, trying to convince himself that his situation was not as serious as it seemed. He would explain everything and they would have a good laugh, maybe share some drinks.

"It's all a big mistake!" Alex shouted back at them from his hiding place.

Alex wriggled beneath the camouflaging branches of the mulberry bushes but they were too small to hide him. Losing his faith in their concealment, he found a drainage pipe hidden among the bushes and crawled inside. The shouts grew louder as he wormed his way deep into the pipe, never for a moment considering where it led. He had to get away from the angry villagers. He could hear their din as it echoed through the concrete pipes, following him as he crawled eventually into a sewer culvert.

"Stop it! Stop shouting at me!"

Alex could hear the shouts of the villagers above him and around him, seeping down through the ground and carried on the wind, a wind that was suddenly fiercer than during his Moped ride. He thought of the voices of the dead in Hades, the cacophony that never ceased. It whirled around him, taunting him. He threw his hands to his ears and willed them to stop.

There in the Underworld, he was suddenly overcome by exhaustion and sank back against the concrete wall of the culvert, shaking from the wet chill and huddled tightly within himself. His fear of capture was compounded by breathing the acrid fumes in the pipe and the uncertainty of the wavering hallucinations that came to him.

There was no way out, he decided, except the way he had come in. They would grab him and throw him to the ground, maybe kick him. They would tie him up and beat him with their farm tools, then lead him off in chains to a stronger prison than the one he had shared with his Navy comrades. Maybe he would be tortured, as seemed to be the custom in this place. It would be exactly what he deserved, for everything he had done in this country, for killing Benson. He might even die, too, and he imagined his parents' reaction to that news: their hard work and all the sacrifices they'd made for their beloved only child, giving him the best start they could on a fruitful career, now wasted in the senseless violence of a wild mob of otherwise simple folk provoked to rage. His odyssey was about to come to a quick and terse conclusion.

A mangy cat wandered into his corner of the sewer, *meow*ing for a rat, and Alex, usually appalled by dirty, sickly-looking animals, coaxed the cat over to him and petted it warmly. The cat, obviously blind in one eye, sidled up to his legs, arching its back and rubbing its ragged, muddy fur against Alex.

He suddenly realized this was something different. Never was Odysseus chased by an angry mob. Odysseus may have traveled to the Underworld to consult with his dead warrior comrades as well as his mother—as visions of his dead grandmother were slipping in and out of his mind—but only Alex survived such an insane ordeal as being hunted by angry villagers and a mad horseman. Seeing the uniqueness of his adventure gave Alex courage. He was not doomed; he could fight back. Or flee to safety.

Alex struck a deal with his cat friend there in the dim light, and the mangy cat showed him the way through the cylindrical corridors. Soon he found himself staring out of the pipe from a sheer cliff that faced the sea. Between his feet, the pipe spilled out its bad water.

He regarded the sea with its swaying waves, whipped up by an approaching storm. Off-shore he could see another point of land, perhaps an island, and he pondered whether he could swim the strait in calm seas. Now was not a good opportunity. With the villagers' enraged shouts from above challenging the roaring wind, Alex considered whether the island he could see belonged to Greece or Turkey. It did not really matter, he knew; he had to escape.

Hiding in the pipe past dusk, he saw the crisscrossing search lights scour the jagged rocks along the shoreline. They were still looking for him. Sure, they reclaimed the old Moped, but now their focus was the need to capture the murderer!

Shaking off his fear, Alex studied the waves. He noted the geyser-like thrust of water below him whenever the waves crashed against the rocks. He counted the cycle of waves, waiting for the least violent wave to return. The only escape route from his cliffside sanctuary, it seemed, was straight down. Somehow.

Alex crawled out of the drainage pipe, stretching his body until his feet found a place along the cliff to rest his weight. With his clothes covered in sludge and his hands dirty and wet, he started down the cliff, rock by slippery rock. Until he lost his footing—

"Ooooh, *shiiiiit!*" Alex cried out, his knees banging against the sharp rocks. He lost his grip and fell, hitting a small outcropping, and landed belly down on a wide, moss-covered ledge that was constantly slapped by the leaping waves.

"Oh—shit," Dr. Johnson groaned, disappointed and a bit angry. "This fucking infection's spread so deep. No wonder he's been going crazy. He should've been healing normally. I need a neurosurgeon in here. This is too complex for me to get into. Get Doctor Lindsay in here. Now! He's going to have to help me clean out this mess."

Alex lurched, stung by a flash of lightning that struck too close to him on the rocky ledge. He had hidden among the rocks, pinned halfway between the top of the cliffs where the constable, the horseman, and the villagers waited with searchlights and radios, and the roaring surf below where angry waves smashed like the fists of Poseidon against the rocks. He was caught, like Odysseus and his crew were while sailing home from the long war, caught between the deadly whirlpool Charybdis and the six-headed monster Scylla.

On the raging wind, a thunderstorm boiled up around him. Throughout the roaring and howling, Alex was unnerved by the wailing sirens of other police cars that had apparently driven up to the edge of the cliffs. He prayed for a block of wax to plug his ears, not wanting to be tempted into giving himself up.

"*Dammit, look*: he's coming out of it! He can hear us. Ensign Joe, it looks like our boy's going to need more juice. Right now! ...He's got to be feeling this. But we can't stop now. Extractor, please. Nurse! I said, *extractor*—pay attention!"

This was the test, Alex knew. The worst possible moment. If he could survive this, he would be invincible. He could prove his invincibility to the gods, and challenge them to set him any new endeavor. His reward would be the hand of Eléna. And her luscious body. He would have her to love for the rest of his life.

Hanging there, trapped between swirling Charybdis below, which would break his body and drown him, and toothy Scylla above, which would ferociously devour him, Alex laughed boldly.

There was no choice, Alex cursed. He would face his death with courage and honor. He would not show any tears, or call for his mother. He would face the end with heroic verve! His fingers grew weary, his arms beyond fatigue, and with a deep breath, he let go—

"He's slipping, Doctor. Heartbeat's slowing."

"Hold on, son...."

"Doctor, he's slipping—now!"

"*That's it*—better give him a jolt."

"Crash cart...."

"Now!"

"We're gonna lose him."

"Hurry up!"

"Stand back, everyone. Ready—*clear*!"

"Hang in there."

"Again—*clear*!"

CHAPTER 20

Alex hesitated, then opened his eyes and saw the bandage once more covering his face.

He *saw* the bandage! He saw the light filtering through it.

He tried to speak, to tell someone about his pain, but his voice cracked. His throat was sore and dry.

"You're awake," a woman's voice announced, noticing his vocalization.

"Where am I?" he asked finally, instinctively turning his head to look around the room despite the bandages blocking his view.

"The hospital," his nurse replied. "On base. At Izmir. The Navy base. You remember? You've been here almost a week."

"No—I don't."

"Nothing at all?"

"What happened? And who are you?"

"You had surgery, Alex. On your eyes. I'm Lieutenant Calloway, your R.N."

"Who—? Calypso? Did you say—Calypso?"

"Who's that?"

"I'm saved," Alex sang out, happily. "I made it back from the Underworld. I survived!" He started laughing, wildly, like a madman. He caught himself suddenly and moaned. "No, I've been cursed."

"What're you talking about, young man?"

"You, of all people, know how the story goes," said Alex. "Caught in Calypso's spell when I was so close to home. So close. I could *see* the shores of Ithaca. I could see them so clearly. I would've been home at last…after ten years of war and many years of my homeward voyage. But now it's all lost!"

He gripped the railings of his bed so tightly that Calloway became alarmed.

"Calm down, young man. Listen, you were out for *seven* hours after the surgery. And you've been mumbling in your sleep for a whole day. You need to remain calm now. You had a bad reaction to the anesthesia. You hear me?"

"Seven *years*? Lost at sea for seven long years," Alex muttered incoherently.

"Okay, let me call the duty doctor."

"I've been held captive by Calypso for *seven* years? Just like Odysseus, I'm held captive by you! No longer a Trojan prince, I'm a wandering beggar who's come home at last. And here's my wife surrounded by suitors. But I must save her! And I have a plan. Athena told me what to do. But first you must let me go! Eléna! I *must* return home. I must find Eléna! I must save her! *Eléna*! I can't let her leave—"

"He's delirious again, Doctor," said Calloway. "He just keeps repeating that name. I guess he thinks he's in some

Greek temple. He's a tourist, I heard."

"No, it's a Greek *tragedy* he's in."

"What do you mean by that? What happened to him?"

"That infection of his, in his eye...." Dr. Johnson's calm voice faded away as he took the nurse outside of the curtains of his ICU cubicle. Alex was listening, hearing every word but was unable now to respond. "It went very deep," Johnson told Alex's nurse. "I was told he washed up on the shore near Edremit. He came all the way from Lesbos, apparently. Somehow, he made it across the strait all right. Then he was beat up by some Turks who found him on the beach there."

No, that's not the way it happened, thought Alex. *I was fighting the Cyclops and saving my crew from the lotos, and fell under the spell of the Sirens....*

"Will he recover?"

"I think so. But he'll never see things the same way again," said Dr. Johnson in hushed tone. "If he's in pain, give him another dose. Let's increase the dosage of antibiotic, too. I'll put in another call to the embassy and see when we can get him stateside."

He sensed them watching him for a moment, seeking a sign that he was finally asleep. A finger twitched.

"Poor kid," said the doctor.

"How about that other young man they brought in last week?" asked Calloway. "The stabbing case?"

"Oh, hell! They're dropping like flies around here," and Dr. Johnson grunted. "Is this a summer travel thing or is it like this year-round? Jesus H. Christ!—stabbings, gunshots, beatings—not a good place for a vacation."

"It has been an active summer, Doctor."

Alex was too numb to move, but as darkness swept over him like a gentle wave, he listened to the words spoken by his care team—words which calmed his heart and gave him hope that everything would work out in the end.

"I'll be glad to get home after this summer duty, that's for certain."

Alex could imagine the doctor staring back at him, as he was finally slipping into a restful dead zone.

"Benson's his name? You mean the stabbing case, don't you?"

"I think so," said the nurse.

"No eye problems?"

"Apparently not."

"Thank goodness."

Dr. Johnson stepped back to the bed and checked Alex's bandage one more time.

"No, that Benson kid," said Dr. Johnson, presuming Alex was already unconscious, "he's going to have to stay a while. I'm not sure how long, but he's going to need more surgery. Stab wounds, you know. They just stitched him temporarily, I heard. Aren't they supposed to be flying in someone for that? A thoracic surgeon. Nobody here good enough for that sort of stitching? Heck, he can't make it on a plane ride home, not like that, not yet. But...I guess he's got nothing better to do the rest of the summer. Kids these days! Anyway, the Turks want to question him when he is recovered. Seems he's involved in some murder."

ꟹ

Someone had been trying to hold open his eyelids, shining a bright light into his eyes. Alex threw his hand up to knock away the light. He heard voices around him, speaking not Turkish but Greek, he recognized. As he tried to sit up, he felt hands urging him to stay down.

"Where am I?" he had asked them, and turned to spit out whatever strange material rose suddenly from his churning stomach.

"You are safe here," a man's voice said. It was deep, rich-toned and thickly accented, but it was none the less reassuring.

"Dad—is that you?"

The man behind the deep voice, somewhere past the flashlight beam, chuckled. "I am not your father," he said, "but I will help you."

"You speak English," Alex muttered weakly. "Are you Turks?"

"No, we are Lesbians," the man replied.

Alex started to speak, then rolled over on the sand and spit up the salty water of the Aegean, remembering how he had been chased by the angry mob of villagers, led by the mad horseman of Büyükkestanelik and the fat constable in an old Ford Impala. Crawling through a sewer pipe and trying to scale a wet cliff in the dark was foggier in his head. Slipping on the rocks and falling into the surf was all too real. Was it only yesterday, or was it a week ago? He could not recall clearly.

"I have to get back to Ilium," he said. "My girlfriend's waiting for me."

"You need a doctor before you travel again," the rich-toned man spoke.

Alex was placed on a stretcher as his benefactor instructed the troop of rescuers. They addressed him as Spanos, so Alex did, too.

Every part of his body seemed to ache as the men touched him, as they carried him up the slope away from the beach. Alex was laid across the back of a wagon and hauled into the town nearby, each turn of the uneven wheels rocking his sore ribs and strained back. It was dark, so he let himself forget what had happened and slept. In his mind, however, lightning bolts continued to strike him, illuminating him in frightening shadows and blazing brilliance.

Alex had scrambled painfully away from the rocks where he had fallen from the cliff. Around the bend in the cliffs, he found a dinghy stuck in the sand. Even though it appeared old and not so seaworthy, he was motivated to test it by the raging mob that followed him along the top of the cliffs, shouting down at him, throwing rocks at him. He pried the dinghy free and pulled it into the rough surf. He had grabbed a piece of driftwood for an oar and paddled his way clear of the rocks. It took all of his strength to move the boat against the rushing waves, but an hour later he found himself out in the currents. He gazed back at the angry people lining the top of the cliffs but was too tired to wave at them. Completely exhausted, he had slumped in the boat, not wanting to rest but unable to continue.

The water soaking his legs soon alerted him that his craft was sinking. He paddled hard once again, but with only half his previous energy, aiming for the point of land and spots of light he saw in the twilight. He quickly used up the last pull of oar his shoulders and arms could bear and sank down inside the boat—just as a strong new current took his boat up on a wave and hurled it toward the shore. Like the hand of Poseidon, Alex sighed.

With the old, weather-beaten slats springing leaks at nearly every dip and peak of the roller-coaster waves, he and his boat were being pushed toward the rocks that guarded the new land. He could see them charging at him but he only had time to grab the oar locks for support before the boat was kicked up onto the half-submerged rocks. The dinghy was split open and Alex was hurled into the dark waters. He struggled to keep his head above the waves—kicking his feet more than paddling with his arms. Stretching desperately for the shore, he grasped the rocks, clinging to them.

Alex had dragged himself up the beach as far as he could, out of reach of the tide, leaving the broken scraps of the dinghy on the rocks.

After the fishermen found him, Alex was taken to the home of Mr. Spanos, the man who spoke English, an old fisherman who had learned the language working on freighters that regularly visited American ports. At first, Alex was too tired and too suspicious to say much of anything so he was content to listen to Mr. Spanos talk casually about his life.

Alex lay in a soft, fluffy bed for a day and a night, then sat up in a straight-back chair for another day, always wrapped in a thick blanket, eating bread and soup, and sipping hot coffee despite the balmy weather. He believed the old man could see his soul was restless, could feel the storm raging inside him, could sense him fighting battles over and over, but could not speak.

The thoughts that drifted through his head during those quiet hours were of Eléna. He had expected her image, pasted firmly in his mind, and the memory of her sensuous voice to sustain him through his odyssey. Now he had difficulty finding her picture in his mind, so he directed his attention outward.

His new abode was a picturesque white plaster walled house with red tiled roof typical of the sun-swept Aegean isles portrayed on postcards. He wished he had his camera, and sighed at the thought that all of his rolls of exposed film were still in his camera bag, left at the constable's station. All of the pictures he had taken of Eléna were there in that bag. His entire Greek vacation was in that bag. Thankfully, London, Paris, and Rome were in his suitcase, back at the hotel in Istanbul—if they were holding it for him still. With the camera bag lost and with it his only pictures of Eléna, it seemed as though his trip were only a dream, something that never really happened. However, with the warming breeze and the fragrant, colorful flower boxes around him, sitting on his balcony perch overlooking the red tile-roofed town, his worries seemed less real and more distant.

Eléna now seemed like the previous night's dream, a dream with shadows that snuck up on him, shifting into the silhouettes of Benson, and Ruger, and Derya and her sisters, and an old motorbike that ran out of gas too soon.

For a few hours each day he enjoyed being among the range of views the wide balcony offered. In his weakened state, yet full of the rich foods and fruity wines served to him, Alex imagined that whatever he had forgotten of the turbulent episodes of the past week were merely dreams sparked by several bad meals. He was ready to tell his tale, as was the custom for visiting strangers in ancient, exotic lands, but he feared his story would be too incredulous to properly pay for all of the hospitality he was receiving.

Maybe someday, once he was back home, he would create a video game based on his adventures: instead of gobbling yellow circles or fighting stiffly animated karate fighters there would be big Turkish constables to fight and angry mobs of villagers to avoid. And a girl to rescue.

CHAPTER 21

"You have been my guest for five days now," Mr. Spanos, his host, addressed Alex. They had finished eating a quiet dinner of octopus stewed in wine sauce, with a salad of yogurt, cucumber, garlic and mint. They had exchanged careful glances, and partook of a profound conversation transcribed in facial expressions and gestures, but no spoken words.

The man invited Alex out onto the balcony for coffee.

"Still you do not speak," Mr. Spanos continued, firing his clay pipe. "You must be filled with a dark secret. I understand this. I am not so curious of your story to force you to speak. It is your business, but I am, as always, a practical man. I wonder what I shall do with you."

Alex faced him, realizing he had not planned to be silent nor impolite to this helpful old man. He simply did not know what to say.

"What do you mean by practical?" he asked finally.

"Practical?" Mr. Spanos chuckled briefly and puffed on the pipe. "You do not see my family about the house, do you?"

Alex shook his head. As an afterthought, he quickly glanced around the balcony and through the lighted windows.

"The reason for this empty house, you see, is that my daughter is away in school in New York City. And my son, he is in college, too: in Melbourne. That is in Australia. They are far away, so I must go out to catch fish alone. A lot of fish to pay for their schools. And my wife...she is three years gone from me. I think of her often. This week she is visiting her mother and father in Crete. That is what I tell myself. She is far enough away for me, yes? She will never return, I know. It is good to imagine things."

The old man laughed uneasily and after a moment Alex smiled at him.

"I'm sorry," said Alex. "And I'm grateful. You saved me, and I don't deserve to be saved."

"Why do you say that?"

"I was in trouble. Over there, back across the strait."

"What trouble could a young man like you ever get into? Was it about a girl? I know from life experience it usually is that."

Alex tried to repress a grin. Perhaps it was a grimace, something born of pain.

"Yes, there's a girl involved."

"Ah! I thought so."

Alex looked away and the house was silent.

"Is there more?" asked Mr. Spanos.

"Yes."

More silence. Mr. Spanos puffed the pipe.

"It's not that I don't appreciate your hospitality," said

Alex, "but…I am *so* tired and *so* sore now, I just want to be a couch potato for a while. I can't say anything more."

"A couch potato, you say?"

"Sorry, it means to just sit around not moving, not doing anything, like a potato sitting on the couch—or sofa, or whatever you call it here."

"Ah hah, I see." He puffed on his pipe, watching Alex. "No, you look like an egg, not a potato. You move this way and that way, almost to fall on your side but you always swing back into balance. You are lucky in that way."

"Yeah…. I guess I am lucky, Mister Spanos," said Alex, followed by a long yawn, "And yet, I feel farther away than ever before from where I need to be. From where I want to be. The harder I try to get back to Ilium…. Oh, I'm glad to be alive, of course—not drowned, or crushed on the rocks, or stoned by an angry mob. Thanks to you."

"And thanks to God," Mr. Spanos added, drawing a cross in the air with his fingers.

"I wish God could deliver a message for me," he said. "If I could at least *call* Eléna and let her know I'm all right, that would be great. She needs to know how sorry I am for what happened. And that I care about her so much."

"This Eléna, she is Greek?"

"Yes—no, American. But Greek. Well, she said she was born in Athens. Her aunt and uncle live there, anyway. That's what she said."

"So you want to tell her how much you love her still."

Mr. Spanos grinned at him for a while and Alex became suspicious.

"I guess so."

Maybe his adventure was all a big joke and this was really Eléna's grandfather. It could be true, the way his weird odyssey was going: with so many double-crosses, hallucinations, misunderstandings, betrayals, the lucky breaks, and fateful encounters. He could imagine his adventure as a movie. His host would laugh and suddenly she would magically appear, walking out onto the balcony to view the stars with him as though nothing unusual had occurred during the past week. He would be quite shocked, of course. Then his heart would explode with joy. They would embrace, followed by passionate kisses—

"I think you must tell her how you feel," Mr. Spanos decided. "There is a god who delivers messages for the love-struck. I know him. He has worked for me, too. Many times. Tell me, do you know how to use a personal computer?"

Alex was not certain what he heard and asked his host to repeat it.

"Come with me," said Mr. Spanos.

The old man led Alex through the house, up to the third floor and into a small den lined with bookshelves filled with souvenirs from around the world.

"I'm not so smart in using it," Mr. Spanos explained, "but I am able to keep in touch with my son and daughter through this machine. I enjoy their news. For that, it is worth every drachma we paid for it."

"You know, I was practically raised on computers," said Alex excitedly, pulling out the chair and lowering himself down to it as though he were entering the cockpit of a jet fighter. "Yes, show me a computer, Mister Spanos, and I can do *anything*: send messages anywhere, get tons of information about anything at all. I've almost forgotten what it's like to be plugged in. For a couple months I've been out of contact with—with *everybody*. Now, thanks to you, I can stop all of this, uh, barbarianism, and reconnect with the world I left."

Mr. Spanos flipped on the power switch and Alex seethed with energy. The magical glow of the screen charged him, and his fingers became like lightning, dancing over the keyboard in a blur of motion, typing out the addresses of websites and databases. He came to TURKEY, then TOURISM, then HOTELS, then ISTANBUL, then the name of the hotel overlooking the Golden Horn where he and Eléna had spent their three nights together.

The hotel's home page showed the front entrance with its Greek columns, French café style awnings, and two smartly uniformed doormen. The sidebar frame had buttons leading to other pages which displayed pictures of the rooms and suites, the restaurant and bar, and its balcony view of the Blue Mosque, and their daily and weekly rates. He recognized it. This venerable, historic lodging was on-line!

"How will you know if she waits for you?" asked Mr. Spanos, but Alex did not reply, his fingers continuing without hesitation.

Alex was busily searching through the source code for an indication of where he could intercept the root directory. With a few changes of code and guessing probable passwords, he was able to access the hotel's guest list. As he surmised, it would not be as deep behind their firewall as accounting information would be. He didn't need credit card numbers; he just needed to see a name. Mr. Spanos soon went and brought back coffee while Alex continued working. Eventually, Alex was able to log on as Assistant Manager Demirsar, using <SEX_GOD3> as the password. Mr. Spanos, curiously studying his guest's computations, had supplied translation of variants on the two most widely used passwords.

His heart beat faster as he scrolled down the screen, checking names in alphabetical order, stopping first at *Apollodorus*. Not finding that name, he scrolled down to *Smith*, her incognito traveling name.

Alex's heart leaped into his throat.

SMITH, ELLEN

The words sat in boldfaced white letters on the royal blue background, underlined as a link to further information. He moved the cursor—a flapping seagull animation that Mr. Spanos had installed. With the cursor over the name of his girlfriend Alex clicked the mouse button. The computer froze momentarily, held in limbo between the guest list page and the page it was seeking. Then the background color shifted from blue to pale green with red text and black numbers in several straight columns. He scrolled down the screen.

As the data unfolded before his eyes, Alex recognized the balance sheet. There were the dates of check-in and of expected check-out, the room rate, lots of service charges, and so on. Had they really eaten that many snacks, drunk that many little bottles of wine, ordered so much room service? His father would faint at the bill.

Alex stared hard at the screen, at the check-out date for ELLEN SMITH. There was none. EXTENDED INDEFINITELY, it read. She was still registered! She was waiting for him, maybe looking for him. She must truly love him.

"She's there!" Alex exclaimed and danced a jig in his chair.

He quickly returned to the hotel's homepage. He skimmed over the mailing address for reservations, telephone numbers for the front desk, international and local reservations, and voice mail, along with the hotel's fax number, teletype number, Internet URL, and their e-mail address.

"Bingo," Alex sang joyfully, and before his host could ask what was so funny, Alex had clicked on the e-mail address and a window popped up to accept his desperate words. His fingertips did not miss a stroke but slipped smoothly through the message:

> URGENT MESSAGE for guest Ms. Ellen Smith, Room 435. I am her boyfriend and I need to contact her. Please tell her that she MUST come to the site of ILIUM the day after tomorrow. It is a matter of life and death. I will wait at Ilium for her. She is my love and my life. I will NOT be able to contact her after tonight so please give her this message. PLEASE!!! Thank you very much. :-)
>
> Alex Parris

He sat back from the keyboard, limp in the chair, exhausted, and took a deep breath, relaxing finally. Only then did he gaze up at Mr. Spanos. They shared a smile.

Alex lovingly regarded the computer screen once more, as though he were kissing the envelope goodbye as he slid it into the mailbox. His nervous finger weighed on the mouse button, then he clicked it and his e-mail message vanished into the electric night.

He remained on guard a moment longer to observe acknowledgement that the message had been sent satisfactorily.

"Let me send it again, just to be sure," Alex insisted.

He clicked the SEND button twenty times before the computer stalled.

A response was coming back, he saw.

"They got it," said Alex, slapping the desk. Then, as though it were a royal decree, he read it aloud to Mr. Spanos, who was looking over his shoulder:

> Dear Mr. Parris:
>
> Thank you for your messages. Please be assured that your message will be delivered to the addressee as soon as possible. No further messages are required.
>
> Hotel Communications Staff

"Is that all you need to do?" the old man asked. He seemed impressed.

"On my computer at home, it takes even less effort," Alex replied, about ready to burst with his renewed ecstasy. "Of course, I've personalized it so much it even recognizes my cough. If you like, I can set up yours to run even better. And I'll show you how to cheat at Solitaire."

"You must be a wizard!"

Mr. Spanos clapped him on the shoulder and Alex winced.

"No," said Alex, "just an Honors graduate of Cal State-Stanislaus."

CHAPTER 22

Long before morning arrived, Alex was roused by the older man, given a cup of hot coffee and cold baklava and pushed into the shower. Dressing in the clothes lent to him out of the son's closet, Alex was hurried out of the house and down the cobblestone streets to the wharf. If they were to deliver him on the Turkish coast by dawn, they must set sail shortly after midnight. They were not too early, Alex noted. The harbor was already bustling with preparations for the day's fishing.

Several of the other fisherman greeted Mr. Spanos, some joked with him about training his new 'first mate.' They climbed onto the swaying boat and, without tending to any of the nets or other fishing preparations, the old man revved up the engines. Ignoring the curious calls of his fellow fisherman wondering where they were going, they slipped out of the tiny harbor.

"Some day I'll make it up to you," said Alex, yawning.

"You can join your woman," Mr. Spanos told him. "That is satisfaction for me. I like to see a love story come to a happy end." He burst out laughing. "No, it should *never* end! Even if it's not happy, your love for this woman will never end, yes? The two of you are forever lovers, yes? You will always work things out."

"I sure hope so."

Alex watched the island of Lésvos grow smaller in the night as they slipped through the quiet waters northward. He saw the town awaken as more lights came on. The sun's ochre spread over the strait and soon touched the distant shoreline with fingers of gold. He sat at the bow, feeling the salty breeze in his face as he gazed straight ahead. The steady chug of the engines relaxed him.

Crossing the five-kilometer strait, they reached Cape Baba where their secret midnight voyage soon turned to parallel the Turkish coastline. Mr. Spanos explained where they were headed: thirty kilometers further up the coast to a point just south of Yeniköy, a small village a short ways inland that was the closest spot to the site of ancient Ilium. The beach there was shallow and sandy, a good place to sail in close. That landing site must be Besika Bay, Alex calculated, where most of the Greek fleet had been beached during the war. The wide, curving shoreline of ancient times had been filled in over the centuries, he knew, and showed no sign of indentation today.

The old man throttled down the engines as they approached Bozcaada Island so as not to draw attention. Once past the island, Mr. Spanos pressed the engines into full service again, forcing it to slice through the waters as fast as they could go. The boat rocked up and down as the waves buffeted the hull.

Finally, Mr. Spanos powered down the engines and then

cruised toward the sandy shore, rocky cliffs rising beyond it. The beach was quiet. He wanted to drop off Alex before anyone saw them, skirting the Turkish authorities in the dawn light.

"This is farewell," said Mr. Spanos, and offered Alex a one-arm embrace. He kissed Alex on both cheeks and wished him a glorious future.

"I'll e-mail you when I get home," Alex promised.

He gathered his supplies, including some fruit and a bottle of water Mr. Spanos handed to him.

"You must walk for two hours or more," he said. "Then you will find your destiny."

The boat drifted toward the shore, engines down to a hum, and Alex climbed over the side, as they had planned. He landed in knee deep water and waded onto the beach as Mr. Spanos pulled the boat back out into the channel. With a wicker pack of food and drink slung over his left shoulder, Alex paused to wave farewell. Then he climbed up the rocks to a high grassy ridge where he watched Mr. Spanos' boat hurry out of sight.

৩

Alex hiked up the coast road a mile, the sea to his left, lit by the rising sun over the horizon on his right. The hill of Ilium was barely in view on the horizon ahead of him. Finding a trail, he wound his way through the mesh of olive groves and wheat fields, and around marshes and scrub bushes, always with the legendary hilltop on the horizon ahead. He felt energized by his proximity to this ancient home, more so by the modern promise it held for him.

Eléna would have gotten his message, he knew. Hotel people were obligated to deliver messages to their guests, and since she was still registered there, his message would be delivered promptly to her room. She would be immediately excited to hear he was all right. She would have to keep herself distracted or she'd drive herself crazy waiting for the bus to take her to him. And, getting his message, she would likely be on the first tour bus to Ilium. That was fine, thought Alex; he would be there long before the first bus arrived. They belonged together, after all, just like their ancient namesakes had belonged together. The gods decreed it so!

On this day, with the arrival of the first tour buses from Çanakkale, gods or no gods, he would know that Eléna wanted him back. He knew he had his quirks, his faults, but the time away from her gave him a new perspective on himself and on their relationship. Less history, more affection. Once reunited, they would begin a new life together. He would certainly surprise his family, bringing her home to meet them. His father would be pleased with her smile. His mother would adore her new daughter. And for Alex, she would fill out his skinny life in California with sensuous ease, helping him make a home there for the survivors of Ilium.

Alex rested on a fallen stone by the Scaean gate, the same place where mighty Hector, the Trojan's hero, had stood defiantly before the Greek armies three thousand years earlier, mocking the weakness of their warriors while Achilles brooded in his tent, stubbornly refusing to fight, all because of an argument he had with Agamemnon over which of them really owned a particular slave girl.

Through this gate also were he and his three Navy friends rudely ushered away. He wondered what became of them, of Carter and his too-young Turkish mistress, and Ruger the hot-head Marine. He thought of Benson and wondered if anyone would ever know what really happened to him. Alex reminded himself it was an accident, plain and simple. And he was defending a girl. He could not dwell on the accident. Instead, he mused about the two days he and Benson had joked with each other, selected moments he would put to memory and the rest permanently erase.

Through this same gate Alex returned triumphantly, awaiting a weary hero's colorful welcome—as some of the locals were setting up refreshment stands and souvenir kiosks, making ready a new day of tourism.

He regarded the first tour bus slowly mounting the hillside, its engine straining, and the next bus not far behind. At the edge of the horizon were two more buses kicking up dust plumes. It was almost nine o'clock, one merchant told him when he asked. He stood to greet the passengers as they filed off each bus.

As he surveyed the tourist lines, he fingered a pocketful of Turkish lira that Mr. Spanos had given him just before he hopped off the boat and waded ashore. It was enough to take him back to Çanakkale, he knew, but not all the way to Istanbul, where he could retrieve his plane ticket and backpack from the hotel. Eléna might be able to persuade the hotel staff to let her bring his belongings with her. Once they were back in Istanbul, he would need to make arrangements at the U.S. embassy for his return to the States without a passport, or have them issue him a new one. He would also arrange for Eléna to return with him. He could probably fit a second plane ticket on his dad's credit card. No matter what hassles still lay ahead, having Eléna with him was all he could ask for, all that he needed to make the end of his adventure perfect.

"You are Mister Parris?" a tall man, dressed in a white suit and black tie, addressed him once the boisterous tourists had disembarked from the three buses and fanned out with their guides. Despite wearing a suit, the man seemed oblivious to the morning's heat. He was accompanied by two similarly dressed men who did not seem too pleased to be on vacation.

"Yes," Alex responded hesitantly. He didn't think they had gotten off any of the buses. No-one wore a suit and tie to go sightseeing here. They were definitely not tourists. "And who are you?"

"We came to escort you," said the man.

Alex seemed puzzled.

"Your, umm, message? About, umm, Miss Eléna? You telephoned to her hotel, yes?"

"I sent an e-mail, but…yes…." Alex nodded.

"She is no longer in Istanbul. We are hired to bring you to where she stays." The man extended his arm casually. "Right this way, please."

"Are you from the hotel?" Alex asked, excited. "The concierge?"

"Concierge…?"

"You know, the guys who take care of whatever a guest asks for. I don't know what they're called here."

The man seemed amused by Alex's explanation.

"Yes." The man grinned at his partners. "We are from the hotel."

Alex followed them over to their car: a large, white Mercedes with Turkish plates parked behind the busses. In front of the vehicle, a chauffeur in a black suit and cap waited. As they approached, the chauffeur went around the car and opened the doors for all of them. Alex beamed, excited by this unexpected turn of events, how he had escaped from his odyssey and made it back to Ilium. Now he was about to be on his way to rejoin Eléna finally—and going in such style, too!

"This is *aaawright*," he exclaimed, sinking back into the plush seat cushions and accepting the ice-cold bottle of beer they offered. "I can't tell you how long I've waited for a nice cold drink like this. Even if it's beer. And air-conditioning."

"Are you comfortable?" asked the man sitting in the front seat beside the chauffeur, watching him in the vanity mirror.

Alex nodded, smiled reassuringly, and took a long, deep swig of the beer. He normally would not drink beer or other alcohol but it was very cold and he was very thirsty. He glanced at the man on each side of him, as if expecting them to be pleased that he was refreshed.

"Fine, thanks," he said. "Aren't you guys going to have some?"

The front passenger cocked his hand at the driver and the car rolled away, slowly passing through the welcome gate of the tourist site, leaving the lost city of Ilium. They turned onto the paved road and drove for a kilometer before the front passenger turned in his seat, leaning over the seat back to face Alex, who quickly lowered his beer bottle.

The man extended his hand to Alex.

"Let me introduce myself to you, Mister Parris," said the smartly dressed man, adding a friendly smile, his teeth white like snow.

Alex took his hand and shook it; the front passenger released first after a too-firm clasp of his hand.

"My name is Michael Mennon-Louis. You've perhaps heard of me? I'm a financier in Chicago: commodities, mortgage-lending, junk bonds, the usual things. I also have other interests which are, shall we say, around the edge of the law. But that's enough about me. No doubt you have a few questions of your own. For now, all you really need to know is that I am the husband of Eléna."

Alex blinked.

"Yes, Alex—may I call you Alex?—I am so *glad* to make your acquaintance, at last. Eléna has told me so much about you; I feel I already know you well. Your kind message to Eléna at the hotel was very considerate. She, of course, wishes to thank you for escorting her on her far-flung travels. She sends her regrets; she will not be joining us. Now I would like to *personally* thank you."

Alex took another sip from the bottle, noticing how white the man's teeth were. He paused in mid-sip, then lowered the bottle. Something just did not fit.

"Excuse me," Alex asked, a bit puzzled. He set the cold bottle between his thighs. "Did you say your name was Menelaus?"

As realization overcame him, the car veered sharply off the pavement and onto a bumpy side road, throwing up a thick, chalky brown whirlwind as they went quickly south.

CHAPTER 23

"This guy's Priority Medical Rescue," Alex heard a man say as he rose to consciousness. "He needs to stay flat. Better put him in the back."

"No shit," said another crewman. "I heard of that before, but I never seen one. What happened to him?"

"How should I know? Read his chart."

The crewman reached for Alex's chart, clipped to the corner of the gurney, beside his head, but could only glance at it a moment before being called away.

"He's civilian...." The crewman's voice trailed off as he left the hold of the aircraft to retrieve more cargo.

Alex was strapped in next to crates of military cargo. He turned his head to the side, to face the sunlight he had for so long only felt. Now he could see it stream boldly through the side window. It did not shine directly on him but it still burned its way into the hold of the aircraft. He saw dust shifting in and out of the shadows, in and out of the light, and he was happy. Heading home at long last, he sighed. And he could see once more, if only with one eye. He guessed the bandages wrapped around his head and over his bad eye made him look worse than he actually was.

The fixed gurney shook beneath him as the aircraft's engines roared to life. Alex held on, even as the vibrations made his head ache. He gritted his teeth through the pre-flight check list, then felt the big bird roll away from the Tarmac. He was more cargo than passenger. That would explain why no-one spoke to him, barely acknowledged his presence. He wanted so much to hear the captain thank him for flying Military Airlift Command from Izmir Naval Base to Oakland, California Army Depot, with stops in Germany and Newfoundland.

He was told what to expect on his impending journey, and even Dr. Johnson came to see him off and assure him that it would be a quiet, uneventful trip this time. Upon arrival, Alex would stay in the V.A. hospital in Oakland for further examination by another ophthalmologist and a staff neurosurgeon before they released him. That would cover their liability, Dr. Johnson said with a sly grin. His parents had been notified, the doctor told him, and they were anxiously waiting to meet the flight, due in at 3:45 in the morning, Oakland time. That news did not give Alex any relief. He had no idea what he would say to them.

As he felt the heavy aircraft lurch down the runway and only at the last instant become airborne, Alex settled in for the long monotony of the flight. He looked around at the boxes and barrels and crates on each side, the bare rafters overhead. He tried to stretch his arms but banged his elbow on the long plywood crate next to him. His limits were established.

He took a deep breath to clear his mind of everything that had accumulated there in the past two weeks, all in preparation for the long flight home. There would be no attendants to demonstrate how to work the seatbelts, show where the nearest exits were located, and mention something about his seat cushion being used as a flotation device. Then would not come the sodas and peanuts, or later a microwave dinner followed by a double feature. Instead, he could either sleep or review the past several weeks of his adventures through Europe, of his odyssey, and reflect on the lessons learned.

Against his will, his mind set its weight on Eléna, carefully forming the image of her face in his mind: her Classic beauty, the dark eyes and the creamy complexion, the great shock of black hair that had wrapped so lovingly around him for three nights. Her hands, neither too soft nor too coarse as they caressed him, as they welcomed him into her world, then into herself. And the full, pouty lips that she had pressed against his, and the promise of passion such kisses held for him. Then the image of her voluptuous figure materialized in his mind, but he sent it away. He almost thought he saw her among the warped sunbeams that showed him the way home, over the land and sea and through the clouds, then above them, up with the sun itself, transported toward heaven, where the gods lived, where he was to dwell.

She would not leave him—not after hours of sleep and hours of contemplation of everything but her. Alex could imagine her arriving home after her own wayward journey. Everything would be just as it had always been, the grounds manicured and clean as she stepped out of the luxury car, her husband at her side as the children ran out to greet her, the nannies and maids staying back but smiling from afar at the tender scene. In his vision, he could not see her face, did not know if she smiled, or if she wore dark glasses to hide the black eyes she had earned from her husband.

Her children would embrace her, probably chanting, "Welcome home, Mommy!" And Eléna would hug them and tell them she loved them, how much she had missed them, how glad she was to be home again. And her husband would echo her words, how glad he was to have her home—in whatever form she remained, just as Menelaus had welcomed Helen back into his palace as though nothing had ever been amiss after the seduction and ten years of war.

And Alex thought of his own return. Someone would be waiting for him, too: his always concerned father, ready to examine his teeth at the first opportunity, and his perpetually worried mother, tearfully embracing him, crying, "My poor boy's finally come home." Her efforts in raising him would become suspect among her circle, and she would doubt her values and her motives over the past twenty-two years. His father, ever the optimist, would remind him: "You'll always go far with a winning smile," but his tiresome voice would no longer believe his own words. With his scars and bruises, his bandaged face and limping gait, he would stand tall on his own and refuse their sympathy.

His mother would weep, perhaps say: "At least you're

alive!" And Alex would snarl, "Yeah, so what?" He would push away their faithful love as something childish he had outgrown. His father would see the chipped front teeth and pour guilt over him for ruining his meticulous handiwork, and Alex would reply, "So what?" Alex would not join in their pleasantries, but bar his soul to their questioning. And his new employer would laugh at his fantastic excuses. Alex would not plead for another chance. He was now handicapped, yet because he had deserved it, he would expect no special treatment.

Fighting his emotions, Alex realized he was gesturing wildly to the beat of his anger.

After hitting his elbow against the crate for the third time, he grabbed violently at the clear plastic sleeve dangling from the end of the crate, tearing it free as some kind of retaliation. He made himself breathe deeply, trying to calm himself, trying to hold back his enraged tears.

What's in *this* box? he wondered, seeking a diversion from his self-pity.

He straightened the flat pouch to read the papers folded inside.

It was a coffin, Alex quickly realized from the military death certificate he saw. He spied the bright red letters printed there: RUGER, KENNETH H., PFC, USMC. His throat tightened. AGE: 20, the papers read.

Alex tried to sit up, jerking in horror against his straps, but they restrained him. He desperately examined the paper through the clear plastic sheaf: Ruger's date of death, as Alex calculated, was two days after his two friends were apprehended in the field. He strained to read further down the page until he came to Cause of Death: HEAD TRAUMA (GUNSHOT, FLEEING AUTHORITIES).

He stared at the official form until they landed in Germany and the box was off-loaded. The crewmen who climbed aboard to carry Ruger's coffin off saw that Alex was awake, staring hard at the papers, but they said nothing to him. He, like the plywood box, was just cargo. The crewman had to pry his fingers loose in order to take the sleeve of papers that accompanied the casket.

As the big plane lifted slowly into the gray European skies to continue its journey home, Alex knew his fate. What really was his fate. He would become a mystery and slink away, hiding within himself. He would cross the River Styx alone, and with pleasure. He would even offer to help row the boat—and he would never look at another woman for as long as he should endure living. When he returned at last to his home, there would be nothing more he could do. His odyssey would be finished, with no suitors to slay or loyal wife to win, no grown son to greet or a kingdom to reclaim. He would not be a king and his name would never be Odysseus—and he would never strive, never seek, never find, but rather to yield always and forevermore.

CHAPTER 24

From the cushions of his parents' sofa, Alex studied the letter in his hands, afraid to open it. He held it up to his eye, trying to see if the handwriting matched the elegant script she had used to write her home address on the Istanbul hotel stationary. After three days, he had analyzed every possible meaning or subtext such a letter could have: the timing of its arrival, the size and type of envelope, the Chicago postmark.

Now he was ready to open it, prepared to endure whatever message Eléna might have sent: perhaps an invitation to meet her in some new exotic location, like Hell, or a lengthy, sentimental apology for everything he had suffered because of her, or a short, quirky note that was all too cute and barely acknowledged the intensity of their brief time together, of their *affair*. That's all it was, he knew. It was never real love. By now, it did not matter to him, so he ripped open the flap, up across the corner where a return address should have been, and whipped out the fancy beige pages.

He read quickly the dark blue ink curling across the

elegant stationary, almost skipping every other word, rushing straight through to the end and lingering on the last page for a long time. He stared at her curvaceous signature.

"Well, what does it say?" his mother asked after a while, stepping cautiously into the living room. He knew she was watching him from the kitchen.

Alex looked up, his face stern and emotionless.

"Nothing. It says nothing." He wadded up the stationary and heaved it toward the kitchen wastebasket, falling short.

She picked it up, straightened it, tried to smooth the pages, and read them.

"She's sorry, Alex," his mother told him, and read on. "After all that you've been through, dear—only a simple apology? She owes you more than that. A lot more. And what's this list of numbers? What's that for?"

Alex sulked, and sank deeper into the upholstery, rubbing away the itch from his good eye, adjusting his patch over the other eye.

"They're bank account numbers, credit card numbers, investments...."

He knew what the numbers were for. In the eternal silences between telling her about Ilium and exhausting themselves in making love, he had told her about his computer skills. He had boasted how he could hack his way into other people's accounts if he wanted to. He knew what he could do with the information she gave him, legal or not. He could drain her husband's accounts, if he wanted. It was difficult for him to type now, anyway, the way his fingers had been broken. But that was not the compensation he wanted or expected.

"Well, you should write her back, Alex," his mother went on. He could still hold a pen, after all. "Ask her what this is all about. You have a right to know. Tell her you demand to know why she—"

"I already wrote her," he murmured.

"You did? When?"

"A couple months ago."

"And…? What did she say?"

He scooted up and, perched on the edge of the sofa, dug into his back pocket. Retrieving a crumpled letter he had been carrying around for a couple of weeks, Alex held it up for her to see.

She came over to the sofa and pulled her glasses from her apron pocket.

"RETURNED: NO SUCH ADDRESS," she read solemnly.

"No such address," he mumbled. "She made the whole thing up."

"Well, we've got to find her, Alex." His mother was adamant. "Your father'll be home soon. Then we'll figure out what to do. We'll get a lawyer—"

"No, Mother. It's over."

"Over?" his mother almost shrieked. "How can you say that? This woman hurt you and she should, at the very least, apologize. A proper apology. Not some quick note on some cheap stationary."

She let the echo of her sharp words come back to her and heard them clearly. Alex gazed at her: the words did not sound like her words, but his. His mother seemed to realize that, too. She calmed herself.

"Well, anyway," his mother started up, "you know you should write a nice thank you note to that doctor in Turkey. Also to that man on the island who helped you. You did get his address, didn't you? And your Navy friend—Benton, is it? When does he get out of jail? Oh, what do they call it in the Navy? A brig? Well, you should write to him, too. That would make him feel better."

She paused, awaiting his response, then glanced innocently around the living room. She did not know what to do with her hands for once.

"I know they'd all like to hear from you, Alex. At least to know you arrived home safely."

Her gaze landed on the writing desk in the corner of the living room.

"I see you haven't sent a reply to Mister Carter's get-well card. Or have you? Forwarded from Izmir, from your hospital. It's been nearly two weeks, dear. I don't see any letters to go out." She sighed. "Alex, you don't want to get a reputation. People notice the little things. Shall I get you some stationary and a pen?"

Alex got up slowly from the sofa without a word, reached for his cane, and hobbled out of their cool, dark living room.

"Young man, don't you walk out on me," his mother scolded, then stopped, apparently realizing, as her son already had, just how hollow the words sounded now.

Alex carried himself through the kitchen to the patio doors, the heaving obesity of despair hanging on him as much as the pain erupting in his busted knee. Sliding the glass doors open, he stepped out onto the bright, sunlit balcony. It was bathed by the same brilliant sun that had beamed down upon him long centuries ago and mere months ago. He choked back his thoughts, no longer wishing to play games. There was nothing of interest for him in wars or conquest. There was no more fighting and history and empires, or even gods. He was ready, finally, to accept that everything was exactly as it seemed.

The end of fantasy had finally come in the scribbled handwriting of the woman he had named Helen: the Eléna who confessed her love for him but her continuing duty to her children and husband. That, he expected. There would be nothing more. What he did not expect was her honesty. Her brutal honesty—recalling in an instant and with sudden clarity the not-quite-so-weak voice with which Eléna had *asked* for help when she found the three Turkish men standing nearby and so conveniently threw herself down in the dirt, just to allow them to help her up. She never *screamed* for help. She simply wanted his attention. Hers was an act which, perhaps innocent in an impulsive instant, served ultimately to restore to her the attention she demanded. She needed to shift his focus away from his ancient obsessions. It did that, he conceded. It also sent him on a torturous voyage of self-discovery that he would have refused if it had come to him any other way.

He tried to see it that way, in order to maintain his fragile balance, but through her too-casual words came the secret of his anguish: the ruse to get his attention, the pretend affront to shake him to rage. *To rage!* She did not know what rage was! She did not know everything that had happened to him after Ilium, only that her husband had met him there and took him for a ride down the coast. She knew how her husband could be, always a jealous man. She could only imagine what must have happened to him, she wrote. For that she was sorry, though Alex was not moved. He remembered the way his hands shook as he examined the letter for maybe the twentieth time. He felt its truth now, its ultimate reality, and wanted so desperately to laugh as he rested his cane against the balcony railing. His throat tightened. Before he visited Ilium, everything was innocence and beauty. After Ilium came eternal truth.

A victim was born every second, he told himself—once more adjusting the Turkish constable's black eye patch on his face—and in every other second a martyr begins to die a slow, lingering death.

Alex stood on the balcony, leaning against the railing, just like he once had done on the cruise ship crossing the Aegean Sea. This time, instead of a wine-dark sea, he surveyed the dry California chaparral on the distant yellow slopes. He held his jaw steady, as tears crept down his cheek, as he dared to recall the torn hills of Ilium, and all the days that fell after—remembering, whispering: *"Sing to me of the man, O Muse, the man of twists and turns, driven time and again off course, once he had plundered the hallowed heights of Troy...."*

Acknowledgements

Any work based on historical facts certainly presumes a bit of research. I have made use of the following texts in the preparation of this novel. Some of the books provided artists' depictions of the places and people of the Trojan War, which often acted as useful aids to my imagination as much as the descriptive text. You may wish to consult them for further information and in following your own interests.

Connolly, Peter. *The Legend of Odysseus*. Young Adult Edition. Oxford, England: Oxford University Press, 1986.

Graves, Robert. *The Greek Myths*. Vol. 2. New York: George Braziller, 1957.

Wood, Michael. *In Search of the Trojan War*. Berkley, California: University of California Press, 1985.

Quotations, references, and commentary to the texts of *The Iliad* and *The Odyssey*, especially in Chapter 9, come from the following:

Homer. *The Iliad.* Translated by Robert Fagles. New York: Viking, 1990.

Homer. *The Odyssey.* Translated by Robert Fagles. New York: Viking, 1996.

Alex's thoughts at the end of Chapter 23 are a paraphrase of the last lines of Alfred Lord Tennyson's 1842 poem "Ulysses".

About the Author

Stephen Swartz grew up in Kansas City, Missouri where he dreamed of traveling the world. His writing usually includes exotic locations, foreign characters, and smatterings of other languages. Strangers in strange lands is the common theme. After studying music and composing a symphony, Stephen had planned to be a music teacher before he decided to turn to English and writing. *After Ilium* was born from graduate courses in Classical Rhetoric and was first put to page in a summer fiction workshop. Stephen now teaches English at a university in Oklahoma and continues to write literary and science fiction late at night.

www.ingramcontent.com/pod-product-compliance
Lightning Source LLC
Chambersburg PA
CBHW050717180626
46814CB00002B/475